# Smile, You're Being Murdered.

## The Immortal Scribe

Smile<u>Final</u>

# <u>DEDICATION</u>

Giving Infinite Thanks to The Most Highest of High Creator and Sustainer of Worlds and Multiverses and their Divine Seven…My Ancestors, Heirs, Family and Loved Ones. AYahShalawam…Islam…Salaam…Oseo…Peace.

The Incarnations and Sagas of The Majestic and Mystical Nobles begins…

Circa 2025

*Immortalis Scriba*

Forever Forward.

# INTRODUCTION:

Icahn School of Medicine at Mount Sinai states that:

"Mercury Toxicity (Mercury Poisoning) occurs when a person is exposed to mercury. Mercury is a naturally occurring metal. Short- or long-term exposure to mercury can cause serious health problems. It's caused by breathing airborne Mercury vapors; Eating contaminated food, especially fish or shellfish — Larger and older fish tend to have the highest levels of mercury; Drinking water contaminated with mercury. Symptoms can include Painful extremities; Tremors; Changes in vision or hearing; Weakness; Memory problems; Fever and/or chills...Diagnosis Your doctor will ask about your symptoms and medical history. A physical exam will be done. Tests looking for mercury may include: Blood tests, Urine tests, and Scalp hair analysis"(Mount Sinai Web.)

Gabby was braiding my hair when she said hold on. She walked over to the white countertop in her usual nonchalant way. I sat watching the Bengals preseason game on replay. "What do you mean come get you?" Gabby snapped. I turned around because although she can be generally loud when she speaks, Gabby was heated! Her toffee complexioned face started filling in with red and I thought her eyebrows were going to form a permanent letter V. "Well, what the fuck happened?" By this time I knew who was on the other end of the phone.

Gabby patted her foot against her white ceramic tiled floor. She dropped the comb she'd been using, and, held the phone in one hand gripping her waist with the other. "That bitch! You sure? Where's the baby? You alright? Hmmm." She spat out rapid fire.

This had to be bad. Real bad. Luckily Gabby had a cordless phone because she covered every bit of her kitchen probing her cherry cabinets for her stashed liquor. "Cling...bing!" She grabbed the bottle of cognac and drinking glasses, I almost thought she was going to break the glass or the bottle she poured so hard. Maybe she noticed my gaze? So, with a smile, she gestured if I wanted a drink. I nodded no thanks. She kept listening.

Turns out, as soon as Gabby hung up the phone she asked earnestly "Freddy's sick, will you ride with me?" I replied: "Sure. Is everything alright?" It was easy putting two and two together to know everything wasn't. "Freddy wants to see another doctor." "Doctor for what?" I was growing more concerned. "He's having trouble walking and his head keeps hurting."

The next morning Gabby and I took off. She was pleasant, but not so bubbly like she usually is. There was a mix of anger and worry in her demeanor. She slammed the gas backing out the driveway. Fortunately the ride up I-75 North was smooth save for Gabby turning the radio off each time a song either she didn't like or wasn't in the mood for came on.

In an attempt to calm her, I asked about her favorite t.v.

show. "You know Freddy's getting divorced now, right?" Gabby switched up on me and emphatically interjected. "Oh yeah? He didn't tell me." I offered cluelessly. "Yeah that chick is off a leash. I told him *before* they got married she was no good. Now he's sick, can barely walk... can't work, she's put him on child support and he's been the sole provider the entire time they've been together-she doesn't work." She finished in a sarcastic chuckle. "I had a funny feeling something wasn't right when Daryl, of all people, called to invite me to their wedding instead of Freddy. While there, I got to talk to him at the bachelor party and he seemed so sure of Regina. He introduced us and she struck me as okay. I mean, I didn't really give her too much thought with everything else going on. I mean, Freddy and I hadn't seen or spoken in like, what, five or six years?"

"Yeah, he told me on the phone. He asked if you'd come with me because he wanted to apologize for all that." Gabby offered. "Really?"

The evergreens and oaks sped by each side of the winding expressway as we grew closer to the small town where Freddy lived. The town basically said "Here I am" as we made our way to the main street through the heavily wooded and alternating farmland. The complex where he lived resembled one of those small camping bungalow's with net-screens for windows. We were in a more rural part of Ohio. Everyone in town seemed to have a gray, metallic silver, or white painted propane tank somewhere in their emerald and spacious yards.

We made a left off the road onto what seemed like an insufficient combination of gravel and dirt driveway which led into a blacktopped parking lot facing the front door of Freddy's portion of what was a wood and stucco; cream and brown stained two-family duplex bungalow. The difficulty of this description should have been an omen for what Gabby and I witnessed next. "Thanks for riding up here with me Mark." I could tell Gabby was trying to keep cool. "C'mon now, we're family." I replied as she and I approached the inclined walk leading to Freddy's place.

The brown door was completely opened behind the gray screen door. The sound of a floor fan whirled somewhere inside. Freddy must've saw our approach, his "Hey-Hey!" burst the silence of what I could only guess a normal day was like there.

There he was. Draped in white. His clothes hanging on for dear life, sort of like those gowns at the hospital that no matter how good you tie them your ass always finds its way out. "Hey." Gabby said quietly. Gabby and I had no idea. The damage had been done. A man once standing six foot one, two hundred twenty pounds and could easily run through a brick wall laughing, dunk a basketball and still beat you in a forty yard dash, was now barely animated flesh. His skeletal structure coerced our attentiveness. Gabby and I both exhaled abruptly when Niecey, Freddy's thirteen year old daughter, entered carrying a food tray.

Freddy's spirit got a little lift while seated in the wheelchair he tolerated as Niecey stepped around him. She placed the tray on his ballooned jeans which most certainly covered his frail and shaking legs. "You sure ain't no fish on here right baby?" Freddy asked suspiciously. "Yes." "No rice either?" "Yes daddy, no rice either." Niecey replied respectfully. "Hi Aunty Gabby. Hey Uncle Mark" Niecey greeted us and went to her room to pack her things.

Freddy managed to get a piece of plain white bread to his mouth. He gave it a couple twirls before downing an entire cup of orange juice that sat next to what looked to be scrambled eggs and pancakes. "Y'all hungry? My babygirl's on fire this morning! Made me scrambled *cheese* eggs and pancakes." We shook our heads no. Freddy must've noticed Gabby and I were still in shock. After calling Niecey back in for another cup of o.j. he lowered his head slightly meeting his right hand and leaned to one side. The plate of food on the tray jittered against the arm rests of the wheelchair.

"Tell us what happened." Gabby cut through the chase. I was glad she did because I know I wouldn't have been so tactful. Freddy grunted and exhaled. His reaction came from a place of such a depth of pain I forced my way to sit down somewhere sturdy in the overcrowded apartment. The people of "Hoarders" would've paid good money for a chance at filming there.

"All I know is one morning I woke up barely able to move.

My head was pounding like Reggie Jackson cracked me a good one. My arms and legs wouldn't stop shaking. Then, all a sudden...it went away. I told Regina and she suggested I call in from work. So I did. Next thing I know, maybe the next day or two later--shit I can't remember maybe a week or two, it all started again. I noticed I had started losing *a lotta* weight, like almost ten pounds a week or so..." Freddy explained looking down at the silverware rattling on the tray.

As if on cue, Niecey came out shyly and took the tray away. This time Gabby followed her back to her room.

"Did you go to the doctor or the hospital?" I asked sensing he could speak more freely with out Gabby present. He knew she was upset. "Hell yeah. I went to the doctor. She sent me to the hospital. They ran blood tests and everything. They referred some specialist, said I had mercury poison." Freddy shook his head gingerly, tears trickled his drained cheeks.

"From where? How?" I was getting agitated. "The specialist best guess was, he said--food." Freddy finished up, inviting the quiet into the small space we occupied.

There was only one way this could've happened. Freddy knew I knew too. Hell, Freddy can't boil water so cooking anything is rocket science to him. "Regina did all the cooking. Outside a peanut butter and jelly or bologna n' *cheese*, I'm in trouble. The Specialist said a little bit a mercury everyday over a certain period a time can go undetected but cause *a whole lotta* damage. Shit. Regina gave me the divorce papers the week I went to the hospital." Freddy panted. "That right?" I reclined into a lump of fresh laundry. "Mhmm. Don't gimme no mo' fish or rice. Noooo way!" Freddy fought to exclaim.

"Well did she get sick too? The kids?" Gabby barked startling Freddy and I re-entering the room. Stuck between aloof and embarrassment Freddy replied: "Nah. Just me."

Freddy motioned for his walker. He grimaced quickly reaching for the walker. "Can't you press charges? I mean, did you call the police? That don't sound right." Gabby asked watching Freddy intently holding the walker in place. "*Police*? I wish. Specialist said it'd be hard to prove it happened on purpose."

Freddy labored to his feet, hunched over, rocking side to side. Just before he could plummet to the table in front of him, I caught him. We managed to a slit on the couch where Niecey slipped his shoes on and Gabby gathered his belongings.

After a few miles of driving, her eyes peeled to the rearview mirror at Freddy stretched across her backseat sleeping. Gabby pulled over, tears flooding her face. "My baby brother! I can't believe this…I'm so sorry, I'm taking you to another specialist first thing."

## Chapter One: Kick Off

See, everything was copacetic before all this Mercury bullshit kicked off. That's usually how it goes, right? My little brother and I dominated the state running the backfield at PHS with Showtime. I had scholarships lined up and was in full swing playing hoop when suddenly Moms passed. From surviving after she had four straight miscarriages, I wasn't fully developed; no ears, urinary tract wasn't functional, and extremely bowlegged; fighting for my life for four months at Children's Hospital from literally inside a bubble. I lost it. Thought I was going to die it was so draining. I became physically sick. Didn't know what to do or where to turn. Lil bro's Mother gave me the okay to stay at their place but in the ball of despair and confusion I chose otherwise. Gabby warned me. But hell, she had a cool gig and she and her dude were basically married. They had a place and I ain't never gonna be nobody's third leg, feel me? So I moved in with Bates and Anthony. Shit, their father Morris was my biological father's uncle or some shit. Whatever it was, we all were kin somehow. Before I knew it, the school year was over and Notre Dame and the other schools had taken their scholarships off the table. I didn't have money to try and walk on anywhere big time so I chose Findlay instead. I thought it would be temporary. I mean, just go there long enough to get my name recirculating and play well enough for the Division One schools to reconsider. I took out a loan and got financial aid. But as soon as I got in the routine at Findlay, the school admissions switched the schools' status making it a private institution. That meant their tuition went way up! It was so expensive that no matter how well I did on the football field the head coach couldn't offer me a full scholarship. As a result, I ended up quitting the team and getting a job just to stay in school. Man I can hear Moms now, "It's okay baby. It's not that deep. You the best." She never wanted me to take things too seriously.

I was always looking out for Gabby's ass. Seemed like I was constantly having to check dudes she didn't want to deal with anymore. Hell, I was the youngest! I remember one time having to walk over to Woodward and check some dude who was a whole foot taller than me! Turns out this cat didn't even know that Gabby wasn't interested in him anymore. However, to both of our surprise, this was only the beginning of this particular adventure I'm about to get into...

Moms, Gabby, and I were still relatively new to Bond Hill. I went to Crest Hills Jr. High and Gabby went to Woodward High School across the street. After leaving the barbershop, I made my way across Reading Road and saw a group of guys hanging out. I didn't think anything of it besides the fact all of them had on New York Yankees baseball caps. I acknowledged them and went about my business. Once I made it to the front parking area of the high school, Gabby strutted over nonchalantly. Her hair was done up like Salt-n-Peppa. She carried her usual grin. I quickly realized her situation was hardly an emergency. I shook my head. "Girl, I thought you said dude was messin' with you?" She smirked. "He was. Ain't nobody trying to talk to him no more." She claimed. "You trippin'. I came all the way over here and you just can't tell dude you ain't interested no more?" As soon as I said that cluelessly, Dan walked over. "Man you better leave my sister alone!" I barked as I basically pointed towards the sky because he was so tall. Dan chuckled as he leaned down over me. "Everything good lil bruh."

I faced where Gabby last stood and she was no where in sight! "Maaan!" I sighed and headed to our cousin Kimbo's house while Dan laughed in the distance.

Halfway off Woodward's property, I crossed paths again with those same dudes with the Yankees' caps. "Those some cool J's man." One guy complimented as the others agreed through head nods and "Mmm-hmms." "Appreciate it." I returned and kept on. "Yea man. I got to get those!" The same guy remarked. Without losing stride or giving second thought I replied, "Swifton Commons is across the street, my dude." "Naw. I need those you got on. Run'em!" His boys surrounded me. It just so happened that we were a few doors down from Kimbo's house. Uncle Ben came out on the porch on his way to work and noticed the situation. "Big Freddy! Everything alright?" He asked. "Naw, they want my gym shoes!" I exclaimed. Uncle Ben reached behind his back with his right hand and returned it filled with his black .38. "Yo shoes?" He repeated. Then suddenly, Kimbo and the rest of my cousins started to exit the front door and stood on

the porch near him. "Nigga please. I'm out." I looked back at the dude who wanted to rob me. He raised his hands and backed away. I walked on while they plotted. "We gonna see you again. Bet that!"
"Fools just don't know. Nigga postin' up like he gone do sumthin'; leaving his ribs wide open." I thought. Ever since Moms put me in those Boxing and Judo classes I had to show mercy to others whom otherwise I'd seriously injure if not, kill.

That Friday I asked Moms about a party Gabby and others told me about earlier that week. "Baby I don't think that's a good idea this time. I had a dream that there's going to be fighting and serious trouble. You might even get hurt. Don't go." She explained. However, my mother left it up to me because she knew I could defend myself. "Ah it'll be okay Mommy! You know I love ya girl. You know I got that whomp whomp for any nigga perpetratin'! Don't nobody want none!" I giggled and mimicked fighting gestures with Bruce Lee sound effects. "I probably won't even go. Gabby just want me there for backup."
I ended up spending the night over Dewayne's. He was my other brother from another mother from church. We were bored so he suggested we go. "We gone go to that par-taaay!" I laughed. "Man you crazy!" Dewayne leaned back towards his room door and shouted, "Hey Ma? Can we go to the party around the corner?" Then he looked over to me and popped his shirt collar confidently. "What Dewayne? Alright Dewayne, don't have me come looking

for y'all!" Miss B warned. "Gotcha! Let's be out bruh." Dewayne said.

We made our way to a ranch styled house just off Reading Road and around the corner from Famous Recipe and Seven Eleven. As we approached the house I recognized Kimbo standing on the porch. "What up cuz? Made it huh?" He said. "Yeah man checkin' thangs out." Dewayne led the way inside and down to the basement of the crowded house. The music was bumping!

As I stepped down on the last stair to the basement, I saw one of the biggest and roundest booties ever! It belonged to one of the most gorgeous girls I had seen since we had moved to Bond Hill. Her name was Dena. However, before my attention got completely lost I noticed a couple guys posted up in a dark corner near a door that must've been the laundry room or something. Guess what? They both had on Yankees hats. I tapped Kimbo on the shoulder. He leaned over so I asked, "Hey man what's up with these dudes in the Yankee hats?" Kimbo's head followed my eyes and he replied, "Them? Oh they the Wild Boys. Don't worry 'bout them. They the little crew to the Renegades. They about 1500 deep all together." He explained. "Renegades?" I asked. "Yeah but don't trip, ain't nobody gone step to us cuz." Kimbo reassured with a wink and head bop. I believed him but for whatever reason my mind thought back to a different occasion when Moms warned me not to go to a certain party in Forest Park after she had a dream about it. I should've listened to her that time. "In my dream somebody got shot at that party in Forest Park."

Now, standing around and checking out the scene at this house party and then spotting those dudes in the Yankee hats, I should've known better. Turns out someone got stabbed and mass police came to that house in the F Section of Forest Park. It was gang related.

The more I tried to vibe with the music and scope out the girls my mind wandered. I downed a forty ounce of Old English 800 and began to let the buzz relax me. However, instead of the good music, round asses, and knockers jiggling all over the place, I thought about the time at Skating when a dude tried to fight the DJ and make him keep spinning records. He wanted to finish slow dancing with his girl. Man, that fool provoked everybody to fighting and throwing chairs. It got so bad SWAT was called in and held everyone outside and forced them to sit on the curb until they spoke to their parents. Cincinnati seemed to be super deep with police back then. Especially deep, whenever it came to young melanated people doing anything related to a good time.

Out of the blue, Dena came over beside me and struck up a conversation. Little did I know that she had just turned down the leader of the Wild Boys and Renegades. "Hi, I heard of you." She said. Prior to this moment I didn't know her personally. "You're new here right?" She continued as she stepped closer and motioned me to slow dance. "Yeah, but I haven't seen you before." I said. I was stunned by her aggressiveness. "Oh I'm in high school." She boasted. "My name's Dena. What's yours?"

She asked as she pressed her body up tight to mine. "Dena? Oh okay, I'm Freddy. You're kinda close ain't you baby?" I nervously asked. Dena giggled and dropped her head. "I don't like those other guys. They've been trying to talk to me all night. Especially him." She turned her head and rolled her eyes at this shadowy figure. All I could make out from the dark silhouettes of the blue lights in the ceiling were two red eyes. The eyes were seemingly human in form. They also appeared to huff and puff wanting to blow something up! "But I like you. Here's my number." Dena said. She pulled out a small piece of paper from her purse, jotted her number down and handed it to me. Still in shock, I took it. She rubbed my chest and kissed me on the cheek.          WHAP! My head jerked to one side. I reached and grabbed for clothes in the direction from where the punch came from. The shadowy figure had emerged from the darkness and the smell of weed strongly bombarded my presence. I held on to his shirt and jacket for dear life. If I had lost my balance I knew I would've got stomped out by others. With my free hand I repeatedly swung, crushing his face with every blow until his initial momentum helped me regain my footing. I kept swinging until all hell broke loose in that basement.

"Let that nigga go man!" Dewayne screamed. He plowed out a pass way through the crowd. The next thing I knew Dewayne had picked some dude up and threw him like a two handed chest pass from off the porch. He, Dena, and I took off for Reading Road! "Huh, Huh…" Dewayne could really move for a big dude! It's seemed like the entire gang was after us. We dipped and dodged side streets, stayed in the cut, and kept away from streetlights as best we could. We didn't take any chances for the gang to follow us home to Dewayne's.

Later that night, I got word from Dena that I had beat down the leader of the Renegades. I was tripping. After that, things really got interesting.

**Chapter Two: Get Down?**

A few weeks before that party I loaned Pete, the wannabe, five dollars. It had been a while and I wanted my money. Kimbo and I were making our way into Woodward's football stadium. It was a big Homecoming game against Withrow. Pete casually walked past and I stopped him. "Hey Pete! Yo Pete!" He turned and came over with a smile. "Hey what's up Freddy?" He greeted. "Yeah man it's been a minute. You got that loot?" I inquired. "I'm sorry man. I'll have it to you first thing Monday at school. I promise." Pete humbly replied. "Okay cool Pete. You know I'm black right? We needs our money mane!" I joked. Pete's face turned pink as he giggled uncomfortably. After he walked away Kimbo and I noticed flocks of people got up from their seats on the bleachers and moved elsewhere. Before we knew it, floods of young and older guys from the neighborhood surrounded us sporting Yankees caps. All the guys acknowledged me with hand gestures or head nods. Besides that they didn't bother us. It was a weird vibe though.

The game was just about to start when I told Kimbo, "Hey cuz, let's sit somewhere else. We ain't gone be able to enjoy the game with all these fools 'round." Then I stood up. "Alright bet." My cousin agreed and we headed to the visitor's side of the stadium. As we walked I got the feeling we were being watched and followed. Slowly, I looked behind me and notice guys in Yankees' caps were

flying out of the Home stands rather orderly and uniformly. A small number of them had even set up casually a few paces away from us. "Man I know these niggas ain't following us." I said to Kimbo. He paused and observed what resembled a well organized strategy playing out. "Cuz, it looks like something's up."
We found new seats but before we got too comfortable, there were Yankees hats in every direction of our general vicinity. Most of the guys were in twos or threes. They sat either two or three rows behind, in front, and or along the same bleachers alongside us. The remaining numbers stood near the stands' exits, the general exits and entrances, and scattered about the progressing crowd. I had had enough. I walked over to the nearest group of guys where Hank was. He and I were cool before the shoe and party incidents. "What up Hank? Why y'all following me bruh?" Hank seemed excited to talk with me. "Oh man! Freddy man, we got you. Don't worry." I was confused. "Don't worry? Y'all got me? Y'all got me for what?" Hank smiled. "Man you beat down Sean! You da man! We got you."
In the distance across the field on the Home side of the stands, a crowd near the concession stand stirred abruptly. All heads turned towards the commotion. "I'm good man. Y'all don't have to get me for nothin'. Appreciate you lookin' out though. I'm 'bout to get into this game." I explained. "You gone get down?" Hank asked. His eyes looked like a deer's in headlights. "Joining what?" I had no clue what he was talking about. "The set

dawg." Hank responded matter-of-factly. "Gang? I ain't joinin' shit." Then I went back and sat down.

"Kimbo, these niggas crazy man!" I told my cousin as I sat down and watched kickoff. "They talkin' 'bout do I wanna join." Kimbo laughed hard. "For real?! That might be a good thing cuz." He continued sarcastically.

Finally, the game was over. Kimbo and I stretched as we stood up. It was a pretty good game. Woodward did pretty good that night but still lost. As we made our way to the exits people seemed to part around us like the Red Sea. I noticed them whispering and pointing in our direction. The closer we got to the gate more dudes in Yankee hats gave me more hand signs and looks of admiration. I didn't know what to do or say except for "Peace muthafucka!" Before I knew it a classmate ran over to me and said, "Freddy did you see what happened to Pete?" I looked at Kimbo who had a blank face. "No." I replied. My classmate continued, "He got smashed. Beat up bad man!" "For what?" I mean Pete was alright. I never heard of him giving anyone problems or anyone having any serious issues with him apart from him trying to act black. "I don't know why man, it's crazy." The classmate explained. Kimbo and I took it all in and walked ahead. Two more Yankees' capped dudes approached us. I recognized one as Ski. He always hung outside Seven Eleven up the street on Reading Road. "Hey Big Fred. We took care of that white boy for you." Baffled, I turned to Kimbo who looked just as shocked as I was. "Say what?!" I couldn't believe what I had just heard. "Yeah bruh. White boy talked shit, talking 'bout he ain't gonna pay you. We handled it." Ski explained. "Man he ain't talk no shit!" I tried to assure Ski but Noni interrupted. "Yeah he did Big Fred. When you walked off he said he wasn't paying you shit so we handled it." I looked with a stupid expression on my face towards Kimbo. He shrugged his shoulders and shook his head. "Man y'all fools crazy. He ain't talk no shit. I don't need y'all handling nothing for me-ya dig?" I barked. I could only guess that Ski realized I had become agitated. "It's cool Big Freddy. Don't worry 'bout it. You gonna get down, right?" Ski looked as dumb as a tire. I sucked my teeth like I had finished a steak at Ponderosa and was ready for a minty fresh tooth pick. "Hell naw I ain't joining y'all!" I shouted. Sadly, after the ambulance took him away, no one ever saw Pete again. He never returned to school. Now, the more I thought about it, the Moon was a deep red on that night. It was full and looked like blood. It was impressive and haunting at the same time.

## Chapter Three: Another Move

One day after football practice at Woodward a tall dark skin man approached me. I didn't know who he was but I noticed he was a regular spectator at our practices. He wore a PHS jacket. I knew what PHS was. They were good. "How you doing? Mind if I talk to you for a minute?" The man asked. I cautiously walked over. "My name is Bradley Pitts. You ever heard of PHS?" He shook his head up and down confidently and smiled. "Yeah I have." I replied still looking for his angle. "Well, we want you to come play football for us." Pitts knew my name, who started over me on varsity, everything. "You ever thought about playing for us?" He asked. "Sure I've thought about it but we don't live in the district." I replied. "Well, let me make some calls." Pitts said while he pulled out his clipboard and pen. "We're gonna have to talk this over with my mother." I assured. "What's your phone number?" Pitts asked. I think it was a couple days later I saw Moms on the phone and maybe a week or after that she said, "I want you to come look at this apartment with me." I was puzzled. "For what?" I asked. She said with a sly smile, "We're moving." I was so confused. "Moving?" I said. "Why? We basically just moved here in Bond Hill Ma." She giggled and said in a playful tone, *"So you can go to PHS!"*

I don't remember lifting a couch, packing clothes, or anything. It was like one day Moms said we were apartment hunting, then the next, we were completely moved in and I was in school at PHS. I was in the Ninth grade. I was inching towards a dream that I always had of taking care of her. Football wasn't my favorite sport but I welcomed the opportunity to be able to attend a more popular school. I loved Basketball. To me it was better being able to perform closer to the crowd unlike Football. Since the days of little league ball with the Tomahawks I knew that I would do everything possible to take care of Moms.

It was the middle of the school year and I was still in shape. Kimbo and I always worked out. I was so sick of struggling that I put my all into staying in shape. All we ate was rice, or syrup sandwiches, or beans. "Moms, I'm gonna get us outta here!" I confidently proclaimed. I was determined to live that good life.

Basically, folks whom I still don't know at PHS or who represented them in some capacity, took care of everything for us. Moms provided no details and I didn't ask. We moved into an apartment complex in Sharonville. I hadn't heard of that area before. I wasn't used to being around that many Caucasians or Europeans like Mark calls them. But we'll get to that later. I felt awkward and out of place. Most didn't speak to me when we first moved out there but as soon as I bought my first PHS jacket they slowly began to warm up.

The shit was weird. I mean like a dream. Here it was I couldn't remember how we ended up in PCS District and it came from what seemed like no where! I compared it to the first time I realized who my biological father was.

I didn't know who this man was although we played together for years. He always came over and tossed the ball or shot hoops with not only myself but also a few of the other boys from our neighborhood. I just thought he was a cool dude. Everyone I knew liked him for the most part. He was like one of those people that everybody knows and he seemed to know everybody everywhere he went. Some folks call those types of people, everyday people. Yeah kinda like the song.

He taught me how to box and always gave me money if I beat him up. One day while Moms was showing me documentation which was one of her ways of teaching me how to become responsible, I noticed another man's name on my birth certificate. It was totally different from the man's name whom I had known as my father. "Oh my God!" Moms repeated. "What's wrong Ma?" She put the phone down. "It's your brother." She said. "Who Terry?" I asked casually. "Not your brother in law, your brother brother." She said humbly. Her head dropped. "What you mean my brother brother?" I picked up the phone slowly. I put it to my ear and said, "Hello?" There was a quick silence and then, "Freddy?! Freddy?" The voice spoke quickly. "Who dis?" My mind was spinning uncontrollably. "Freddy where y'all at? I'm coming to see you." I told him what I knew about our location. Soon after we arrived in Sharonville we were quickly moved to The Colony in Springdale. Ceville got there in about an hour. He had no clue that he had a blood brother either. Our father and our mothers had issues amongst each other. The more I learned about our family the more I just wanted to do my best to take care of Moms and my sisters. They were really the most consistent people in my life during those years. Their presence was consistent. The way I could rely on them being their true and authentic selves. You know what I mean? They didn't put on and didn't make me feel like I had to put on some mask to be accepted. We just did us. You feel me? Despite how hard or challenging life was and from what I can look back on now or about to become those bonds were the inspiration that fueled my drive for success. The kind of success that's sustaining and long-lasting. Not temporary and shallow. I wanted to make them proud and made sure they understood how much they meant to me. I was going to succeed no matter what just for them.

## Chapter 4: Back To 513

When I think back on how I walked back from the Barbershop that day and bumped into those gang dudes, plus later on how somehow I became their leader, I remember seeing these other two dudes who had bloodshot eyes as well. Their eyes were so bloodshot they were way past what drinking or smoking could do. They didn't look right at all. They stood across the street and eyed me the entire time I approached the other gang members and shortly thereafter. They didn't flinch at all even when my uncle flashed his piece. Come to think of it, I think I remember seeing one of them whispering in Dena's ear just before she walked over to me and started talking. Maybe that's why I didn't feel like hollering at her. I mean I saw her when we first got to the basement and she was talking to her girlfriends. She laughed a little and had a cute little twinkle in her eyes. But after that dude walked away from her and she approached me, her eyes were blank. Just black. As we stood closer together on the dance floor, I got to look deeper into her eyes and there were these red squiggly things moving around in her retina and pupils. Shit was weird. Now years later, it causes me to remember when my little brother told me about what had happened to him while he was messing with this girl who ended up becoming his baby mama. As a matter of fact, he had already heard about these dudes. He told me a story about how he found out this chick he was messing with seemed to have mass different personalities and did strange things whenever she came back from visiting her relatives. Her mother especially. Mark, my lil bro, said the shit got crazy after he came back to The Nati from after moving his moms and the rest of his people out to Cali. That little nigga wild! See, I had my wild ways and for damn sure not scared of anything but I'm a lot more laidback. For the most part he's pretty quiet, hardly says much. However, Mark's the type that when he does talk, he says what people are scared to say or try to be polite about. He lets you have it raw! And he's ready for whatever if you can't take it. Shit makes me laugh. Little did folks know at any given time bruh might've had a pistol, knife, nunchucks, whatever on him. He was so quiet about things the shit kind of scared me because I have no doubt that if the situation called for it, he had no problem using any of those "tools" as he calls them. I've had to keep the peace between Mark and others several times but that's my dude. He doesn't start trouble and he's never afraid to call bullshit when he sees it.

He got that from his moms'. She kept a .380. I remember one time when she was visiting my mother and they were cracking up laughing about something they were talking about. I asked, "Mama Kendra what's so funny?" "Baby some lady at the church got to running her mouth about what she'd do to me. And, I guess she told her husband and he got all bent out of shape and approached me." I was like, "For real?! Why he ain't let his wife handle her own? Was he bigger than you?" My mother dropped her head and started giggling. She shook her head side to side and closed her mouth tightly while trying not to bust out laughing. "Honey, I ain't worried 'bout nobody out here!" And she and my mother both shook the kitchen they laughed so hard while she lightly patted a bulge sticking from out her purse laid casually across her lap. "You understand. Don't you?" Mama Kendra asked with her bright smile. "Yes ma'am!" I answered swiftly.

Anyway, back then, Mark and his homeboy Amir were always cracking jokes and talking shit whenever they came around. They worked hard too. Mark is an Engineer and Amir owns a remodeling company. I'm proud of them both. As bold as they are they could easily be in the grave or locked up because they're just alike. Highly intelligent, fearless, and honest. I'm not going to say too much about Amir except he's good people and -don't test him.

Now it had to be just before Mark was about to move to California when he started telling me about this chick he met. See, Mercury poisoning messes with the memory something terrible. I lost of a lot of time after I began treatments but we'll get to that.

Anyhow, I was worried about Mark. Up to that point he hadn't made the best choices in women. I can't say it was all his fault though. He's just one of those people with a big heart and, as far as women were concerned in those days, he treated the wrong ones too good in my opinion. Anyway, this was at the height of the Mercury damage feeding on my body. Mark and Gabby came in town to pick me up and take me back to Cincinnati. Funny how The Spirit works, isn't it? I mean, Mark and I hadn't spoken for a good while. It just so happened that the day I decided to call Gabby to ask her to come get me he was at her house!

We spoke briefly over the phone. I believe Gabby was braiding his hair. But anyway, as we started catching up, he got to telling me about these two dudes he had seen at this chick's mama's house. He said, "Bruh, this chick got some gruesome lookin' folks in her family! Man, you know I don't like speakin' on nobody's family but damn! These fools look like they was possessed. Eyes all deeper than blood red and they had the kind of squints in they eyes when they smiled that made me put my hand on my heat Bruh, for real." Mark explained. "You brought yo piece inside her mama house Bruh?" I don't know why I asked but I did anyway. "Hell yeah Bruh! The Zone done changed." I chuckled a bit but understood full well he was serious. "Was they some kin to her?" I asked curiously. "Guess so. The crazy thing is I had seen them before and each time I had I heard bad shit happened that day or that night. They don't look all the way Human bruh…them Niggas look like demons." Mark explained. "Ah Bruh they can't be that bad. What's they names?" I asked. "Sama and Ib or some shit. I ain't fuckin' wit them niggas Bruh. Anyway…you coming home right?" Mark changed the subject and I didn't think anything else about it. Maybe a few days past and next thing I knew we were in Gabby's car headed back to the 5-1-3.

While we were in the car I thought I poke fun at Bruh a little. Sometimes I like to say certain things just to hear his reaction; shit's funny as hell! "Hey Bruh, how's Holly doing?" Mark gave me the side eye but said nothing. I tapped on his left shoulder from the backseat. "Hey Bruh, you hollered at Holly?" I repeated. "Man whatever." He responded flatly. "Hahahaha!" Gabby and I laughed so hard while Mark turned up the radio. Suddenly, I realized I was finally escaping the deepest rut I had ever been in. The further we traveled from Fostoria, the more weight I felt lifting from my back, chest, and soul. Before I knew it, my eyes were getting heavy. My heart was getting lighter. I hadn't felt comfort like that in years. Just being in the company of Gabby and Mark seemed to work wonders. I knew I was way out of harm's way. I took the pillow Gabby had on the floor and put it against the door on top of the armrest then stretched out across the entire backseat. Honestly, after experiencing such euphoric relief from getting away from that evil bitch for good, I should've waited and enjoyed the moment a little while longer before asking Mark to fill me in on his situation. I'm grateful he didn't let his guard all the way down the way I did. I folded my arms behind my head and enjoyed the mix of the Reggae music that was playing from the cd player and the hum of the car's tires against the road. "Nah, for real Bruh. How you doing? What happened with that Bria chick you started telling me about?" I asked. As he began speaking it seemed like he was describing a movie. Everything was vivid and quite honestly, unbelievable. But the more he spoke, the more anxiety started to rise in my gut. I don't know. It was like he was connecting dots from my life I had unsuccessfully tried to connect. My point is that both of our mothers had always told us how the Spiritual World and demons were real but we never thought we'd actually have to deal with them. At least I didn't and not that close in person! As soon as he mentioned those two dudes I should've known better. Let me be clear here, I'm not saying that all the people in Fostoria are demons. However, I should've recognized those demons while they hung out at my bachelor's party. Fostoria is so small that basically most of the town stopped by Regina and I's house and wished us well. Hell, seemed like half of the so called black people up there were related to her. Somehow as I sat out in the yard with Mark, the kids running around and our boys drinking and having a good time with the soon to be bridesmaids, I knew something wasn't quite right. Sure, I wished Moms was there but that wasn't all of it. Mama Kendra wished me well but wasn't feeling Regina. She hadn't even met her. Mark was Mark. He's skeptical and protective by nature but he didn't say anything negative.

The Sun shined warmly, just right. I checked out the top of the backseat's headrests and scattered Gabby's knick-knacks around the rearview window. I couldn't help but to think of how many cars she had had throughout the years. Yellow rays warmed the joints of my aching knees and seemed to ease the blood circulation through my legs and feet. Slowly, I crossed my ankles and watched the trees and occasional buildings roll by through the backseat window. Mark's words sank in just as my head did against the pillow…

## Chapter 5: Fresh Paint

The Summer heat was mild. A gentle lilac breeze filled the air; traffic wasn't too bad for this time of day. And, everywhere there were families and friends grilling out. Mark had just finished remodeling his three bedroom starter house in Woodlawn with his homie Amir. After more than six months of fixes, updates, painting, and loud repairs Mark felt like he had a brand new home having wiped clean any trace of his recently deceased sister. To add to his satisfaction, statued, he proudly stands taking it all in.

The thick carpet of Kentucky Bluegrass lawn ruffles gently now fully recovered from the damage his distant cousin, three teenage children, dope selling baby daddy who got her hooked, and filthy pit-bulls. Mark had no idea of the varmints occupation. Needless to say, the red brick; windows; gutters; and shingles of the Texas style ranch house had been in dire need of attention. The trampled sage planted below the cream trimmed front bay window managed to peek a whiff of aromas mixing bar-be-cued everything. Spices, sweet potato pie with fresh brown and white paint throughout the cul-de-sac.

Mark couldn't believe it was the same house. "Man oh man looks good" he said to Amir. "Yup, smell good too. Hey man we did good, let's go next door and eat." Amir replied as they both smiled and slapped dap. While Amir headed towards the immaculate front lawn next door attached perfectly to a two story white house with orange trim and gutters, Mark looks over his landscape complimenting his mother's tastes in Evergreens and yellow and peach roses. Looking past their recent neglect he finds enough gumption to inhale. His eyes closed, a smile filling his face with the 3 o'clock sun. "Just gotta put these tools in the garage man!" Mark calls out to Amir whose anxiously glaring over at him standing by the Thomas's side gate. Laughter bubbles over bumping music and rattling the metal gate displaying a hand made cardboard "COME TO BACK" sign. Pacing back and forth, rubbing his hands like a hungry fly, smoke clouds flowing amidst him between cars and trucks packed tight to the top of a closed two car garage... Amir's barely in view. The chocolate garage door handle turns and unlocks. Mark's ashy hand lifts the door, the other holds his Craftsmen tool belt and drill. A decent amount of vacuum releases with a surprising stench. Mark shakes his head abruptly on contact. The only thing Mark has left to completely clean now is this garage. It caused most of the inside of the house to wreak of dog shit and urine. Until now, today, Mark felt good he, at least, got the entire first floor of his house back together with new paint plus the outside and in all the rooms. He completely restored the kitchen with appliances and fashioned a modern bathroom with a corner styled marble blue jacuzzi featuring a 13-inch over hang television paired with Alpine speakers recessed into the aqua green ceiling. Chrome fixtures highlight the master's bath including dimmer lighting and matching Blu-ray player. "Guess it's really true...business and family don't mix." Mark observes disgusted, exhaling sharply to himself. He carefully places his tools on top of his sister's broken washing machine frowning almost slamming the garage door shut.

Rolling up the main strip everyone calls Springfield Pike the neighborhood felt polished, new, and refreshing. Mark was slowly beginning to realize he was back home each day and didn't feel as refreshed as he did back in Cali where he spent the last five years. As he headed out enjoying a comfortable recline of leather interior still whiffing brand new, a slight grin graces his usual stone face touring the dismal streets he once knew. His waxed clean blur turns left towards the Half-Price Bookstore, his new hangout since all the Black owned bookstores were forced out of business by the large chains and Internet. In Mark's opinion, the independent stores closed due to the fact brothers and sisters don't read much outside of mainstream titles nor supported each other, especially where he's from.

Mark had his mindset on finding something good to get into. His plan consisted of a good read, getting a veggie lovers pizza, beer, and a movie then enjoying his first weekend in his 'new mansion'. The twelve inch subwoofers pulsated violently in the back of Mark's customized onyx Escalade while approaching the bookstore plaza. He even cracked his limo tinted windows which was a little uncharacteristic of him. After being in Cali for so long, Mark felt like a stranger in his hometown and didn't want to be seen. His mother unsuccessfully encouraged him to stay and not return to Cincinnati. Still coping with the mysterious murder of his twin sister Melody, found hanging from a ceiling fan with her hands tied to her back with gunshots to her head and chest, he trusted few. There were no witnesses. Mark became a beneficiary of a sizable inheritance. He didn't want anyone from outside his neighborhood to smell the fact he was back and had come up on — Pacific deep pockets.

Back to reality:

It was rumored Mark and his family always had it. Good standup people. Hustlers with big hearts. "Haters everywhere…" he said as he pulled up to the traffic light on Princeton Pike at the relatively empty intersection. Two familiar faces sporting baggy dark clothes and flashy necklaces gawked at his thirty-two inch chrome rims beaming reflecting the street lights with a thirsty look in their bloodshot eyes. Unimpressed, Mark pats his pistol resting comfortably on the passenger's seat. He acknowledges the two thugs by gesturing his head up even though they can't see him. "Vrooom!" The perfectly tuned V8 hums as the light changes green. He pulls off driving a little ways further then turns left in a slightly full plaza parking lot on the side of the building. The Escalade slows next to a well lit alley adjunct to a bank. To anyone with sense, his strategy was perfect. He didn't have to keep an eye out for jackers nor on his truck because "Fools ain't gon' fuck around next to no bank. Not out here anyway." Mark assured himself and swaggered towards the bookstore door. He politely held it open for an older couple as they exited and thanked him.

## Chapter 6: The Purest Of Evil

"Nigga ridin' clean ain't he?" Sama says to his comrade glinting a scowl in the direction of the Escalade. "Yezzah, indeed. He bedda watch his'self." Ib returns just before coughing up red phlegm and spitting it on the sidewalk where he and Sama stood waiting for the bus. "You know who dat is right?" Ib asks still eyeing the cracked open tinted window. "Mmm-hmm. Fa sho'." Sama replies confidently, "And he bedda hope he don't catch it like his sista." He finishes with a smirk. The two of them giggle like hyenas just before the light changes and the Escalade pulls off. They examine the shiny SUV until the bus blocks their view.

The bus stops with a shhh. The door opens and the driver nonchalantly watches the two slowly get onboard with inebriated steps on the way to pay their fare. Eyes of the half full bus glance, some pause, no one stares. It's more than obvious Sama and Ib are not to be tested and will cause physical harm at any moment.

They find facing seats at the middle of the bus. "Man dat bitch thought she was gonna get away without spreadin' dat wap!" Sama begins through a murmuring barely audible and only understood by Ib. "Ha! Sho' did! It was good too, til she tried to jump bad and bite a nigga…" He says rubbing the flimsy skin slightly growing back over the gash plug on his neck just beneath his hoodie. "Prolly would'na blasted she'd not done it." Ib adds still rubbing his neck with a look of possibility on his light brown scarred face. "Shit fool you woulda blasted anyway. She already gave up da loot!" "Uh—you right." Ib confirms and they giggle like real gremlins a little harder than before.

The bus' engine sounds as it rolls up the street passing Tri-County Mall on the opposite side of the street behind the window where Ib sits. Sama and Ib, caught up in the amusement of their hideous exploits, pay no mind as the bus heads to the next stop four blocks up.

"Thank you, young man. Your parents raised you well." The elderly woman says to Mark as her husband smiles in approval. "You're very welcome. Y'all take care." Mark says as the couple completely exit. Entering the store he turns to his right to take a slick look out the window facing the street to watch the bus speed down the road. He begins to feel more at ease but remains on point as he enters the bookstore. "Man, you never can tell where some bullshit is going to pop off." He says to himself.

The aisles of the store don't look too crowded with people this particular evening. The clerks seem to be taking things casually while they return and pick up books to and from their shelves and carts. It's the vibe that a bookstore should be. Laidback feel good energy. Whatever peaks your interest is there for the taking! As much as you can handle. Mark is loving this...

"You have a good night ma'am." A portly older woman carefully steps down the bus' stairs gripping the handrail. "Why thank you. I'll see you next time." She replies

managing to make it onto the sidewalk. Car headlights
flash nearby. "Oh there he is." The old woman waves and
walks in the car's direction. "Careful now." The bus driver
with perfect posture sits up and waves in the woman's
direction and the car honks again. The bus driver's smile
slowly fades to a scowl as his eyes turn up to his
passenger's mirror. "Mane I wish this ol bitch hurry like
da fuck up. Got shit to do!" Ib calls out. Sama cracks with
laughter. He rocks front to back in his seat. "Fuck you
looking at? Get dis muthafuka rollin' mane!" Ib continues.
"Don't talk to me like that sir. That kind of language is
grounds to get removed from the bus." The Bus Driver
responds. Sama's hand slowly reaches towards his
waistline. "You must not know who we are? Yo kinda lang
witch is ground to get you in da ground, ya feel me?" Ib
spits. DONG! A passenger breaks the silence pulling for
his stop. The Bus Driver screeches to the stop and opens
the door. He rechecks the passenger hopping off safely,
faces forward, and remains facing forward. The knuckles
of both his hands crack white as he merges the bus back
into traffic. He wipes his brow with his forearm. The bus
engine roars. Ib's red eyes lock on the Bus driver through
the passenger's mirror. "Play wit'em" Ib whispers. "Play
wit'em." He repeats. "Play wit'em." He chants. Sama
removes his hand from his waistline and begins to slowly
rock from side to side in his seat. He giggles. "Play wit'em,
play wit'em, play wit'em'…" Ib continues chanting. Sama
cocks his head to one side and while rocking then slowly
raises his right hand. "Play wit'em." The bus driver leans

forward like he's in a high speed chase. He glances up quickly into the passenger's mirror. "Play wit'em." Ib goes on. Sama now has both hands motioning and moving like he's flicking moisture or something from off of his fingers. "Play wit'em." Cars begin honking and swerving on both sides of the bus. "Play wit'em." Sama hands and fingers flicker faster and faster. The bus driver's sky blue shirt is soaked with sweat down the middle of his back. "Get out of the way!" The Bus Driver screams. "Play wit'em." Ib repeats. Sama makes one last strong and big motion with his hands and fingers in the direction of the Bus Driver and then lets out an inhumane cackle. "Please, people!" The Bus Driver slams on the brakes. Sweat pours from all over him. He desperately reaches for his bag nearby and pulls out an inhaler. He takes several quick pulls. DONG! He looks to his right as the bus door opens but no one is there. He slowly glances up at the mirror and Sama and Ib are nowhere to be found. The LED advertising light blinks and makes static sounds then blasts electrical sparks above seats where they sat.

## Chapter Seven: Behind The Times

Once inside, Mark looks over the popular book ends and end markers full of book titles. "Only so called white folks read that kinda shit." He says to himself with a sigh. He strolls along the corridor and aisles of bookshelves overflowing with reading materials. "Gotta get to my spot" he says to Tim, the store manager. He and Tim have become familiar during Mark's many visits since he's been back in town. "I hear ya Mark. Well, take your time, it's good to see you again. We've got some new inventory I think you'll enjoy." Tim says just before another customer walks up to check out. "Right, right. Cool Tim. Thanks. I'll check'em out." Mark replies and continues on to the Metaphysical/Spiritual section.

While in route scanning the shelves left and right, Mark sees a big booty bursting out the jeans of a woman whose bent over checking titles on the bottom shelf of the History section. Mark slows down just enough to see the top of the woman's pink panties and her caramel colored skin in between the bottom of her shirt; leading to her panties. Mark coolly approaches the apple bottom and the beautiful woman senses his presence and quickly stands up straight. "Hey Mark, I didn't know that was you! Whatcha doing up in here?" Mark smiles brightly recognizing Bria, a recent acquaintance from the study class Mark started attending when he first got back home. "Yeah, I'm here checking out what they have new up in here. You're looking nice this evening, almost didn't recognize you." He grins. Bria gives a playful look of shock then says, "What? So what you're saying is, I don't look nice all the other times you've seen me at class?" Mark chuckles in his cool way. "Nah, my bad, didn't mean it like that. You always look good. It's just today your jeans really got my attention." He says trying to take his foot out his mouth. "Mmm-hmm." Bria says as they both laugh loud enough to realize they're inside a quiet place. They immediately lower their voices and continue…"So whatcha looking for today Mark, something for class or?.." Bria inquires turning slightly to the side to continue her book search. "I don't know, just seeing what grabs me in the Metaphysical/Spiritual section." Mark replies while watching Bria. "Oh okay, I see." Bria says, her eyes scan the shelf in front of them. "Are you looking for something special or in particular because you were way down in there!" Mark says smiling, almost mimicking Bria. She spirits out in laughter again but instantly covers her mouth. "Shut up! I wasn't doing all that! No I'm not looking for anything in particular but, it's like they always put the books written by Black authors on the very bottom shelves even though they say they're supposed to be in alphabetical order." Bria states matter-of-factly. Mark nods in acknowledgement. "Yeah. You're not surprised, are you? I mean, look at where we live and the history of this place. Even Mark Twain back in the 1800's said quote: At the end of the world he wants to be here because it's always twenty years behind the times. Something like that." He finishes with casual confidence.

Obviously impressed, Bria's eyes sparkle with revelation. "Wow that's deep! Even though he was a cracka, he was definitely right about that." She continues. "Yeah." Feeling himself getting too close, Mark responds smoothly. He holds back from furthering the conversation. He starts walking away: "Well it was good seeing you outside of class. You take care Bria." Bria steps toward Mark. "Dag Mark, you don't have to go so fast. Let me see what you find over there." Bria's smile and curious demeanor wins Mark over—for now anyway. "Cool." Mark replies as they walk slowly, almost stride for stride to the Metaphysical/Spiritual section.

Mark and Bria carry on conversation like neither ever have before. Their chemistry is ridiculously good, like they've known each other from a previous life—or their entire current lives'. To both of their surprises they talked so much and so long that the store closes before they realize they haven't bought a single book. "Hey, why don't we go to their other store on Colerain Avenue? They stay open longer." Bria suggests. "Okay if it's cool with you and your man?" Mark adds smoothly. "Him? Shhh— please. He and I are on the outs. We live in the same house but we don't sleep in the same bed or keep the same hours. I'm ready to move on." Bria explains. "Or it appears that way. I hear ya' sista girl." Mark thinks to himself. He hesitates about pursuing Bria romantically. Reluctantly, he agrees to meet Bria at the other bookstore. "Sure. That's cool. I don't wanna cause no trouble where you rest your head though." They exit the bookstore parting for their separate vehicles. Turns out Bria was parked near the store's front door. "Man Bria, you got the best spot out here." Bria turns and chuckles at Mark. "Shoot I got lucky. This lady was backing out soon as I pulled in. You know I had to swipe that!" Bria returns. "See ya' in a minute." Bria finishes as she unlocks her champagne colored Honda. Mark gives her deuces just before disappearing into the slight shadow between the store's lights and the banks parking spots just before the bright light beaming down on the corner of building over a walk up ATM.

## Chapter Eight: Flags On The Play

By the time Bria and Mark got off the freeway night time traffic had picked up with travelers who were out enjoying the summer night's breeze. They rolled with the tops of their cars back or windows all the way down. Mark drove behind Bria. He noticed how fast and careless she handled her car. Apparently, she was unconcerned about running over pot holes. She didn't attempt to swerve nor avoid any of them that Mark did when they popped up on the road. "Damn this chick don't care about her car at all!" Mark said to himself as he easily cruised and avoided anything that would make his travels bumpy.

They finally arrived at the bookstore and parked in front of each other adjacent to the main entrance of the Half-Price Bookstore on Colerain Avenue. Bria popped out of her blue compact car and started walking toward the driver's side of Mark's truck parked behind her. Mark, hidden behind the tint on his windshield checks out Bria's voluptuous frame and young blemish free face. He's attracted.

Mark notices, but doesn't take heed to the detached look of confusion in Bria's gathering eyes. She steps out and, as if on cue, picks up on their conversation as Mark opens his door then rolls up the window. "I like your truck Mark." Bria compliments while looking over Mark's onyx and chrome latest model Escalade. "Oh yeah?" Mark says appreciatively. "Thanks Bria. It's fully loaded." He allows the door to close on its own and they walk side by side into the store. The tail lights of Mark's truck blink brightly twice as he sets the alarm casually with they key fob held in his hands unseen.

Once inside the store things seamlessly picked up where they left off earlier at the first store. Mark and Bria began creating a bond but something is causing Mark to feel uncomfortable. He doesn't trust the vibe between Bria and himself. It's not so much Bria as it is his life in general. However, it's complicated. He knows it's something about her that he shouldn't trust that's completely separate from his past experiences. But Bria's so friendly and easy to talk to. She's a definite sweet heart, although confused and down right twisted about more than a few things that Mark is still trying to put a finger on exactly. Right now though, Mark's just following his spirit and staying in the moment; just like Brother Rahim talks about in class.

"Man, time is flying!" Bria says pulling out her cell phone checking texts. "Yeah it is. I gotta get ready to dip." Mark says relieved. "Oh so you just gonna leave me huh?" Bria teases with a grin slightly revealing an open faced gold tooth; her thumb texting in a fast deliberate motion. "Yea gotta a few things to catch up on. Plus looks like your man needs yo attention." Mark says sarcastically causing Bria to instantly stop texting and review his face for a smirk. "Oh for real?" Bria shifts her weight over to one leg placing her opposite hand on her contoured hip. Mark doesn't blink. In fact, after a few blank seconds he motions to walk away leaving Bria standing there, her bewildered eyes following. "Oh Mark don't be like that. I don't want to be with him. We don't even sleep in the same bed. He's always gone until late. We haven't had sex for months. I really want out but I don't know how to leave him. He doesn't have a job and the apartment's in my name." Bria breaking her pose abruptly grasping for Mark's arm but somehow finds his hand. "Look Bria I don't want no trouble and I definitely ain't trying to break up nobody's home. I'm sorry to hear all that but that's your business. If you don't want to be with the dude — leave. Or, tell him to move out. Either way — I'm good sister. You have a good night." Mark caresses Bria's hand hoping she doesn't have any hard feelings for him being honest. Somehow he musters up the courage to let go of her hand and force his eyes from peering into the longing he senses developing between he and Bria. "I promise Mark. Steve and I are not fucking. I don't want to be with him."

Mark hands the woman at the counter a $20.00 bill and waits fighting the feeling to stare into Bria's hazel brown eyes. He swallows air. Gulping and exhaling wishing he had a brew. Bria watches both he and the cashier patiently. Her eyes and nipples call for Mark's attention and embrace. The pheromones are so intense the cashier swiftly hands Mark back $5.23, her eyebrows nearly forcing her glasses off her nose before she musters "Hmmp!" Mark respectively takes his change and thanks the cashier. He calmly turns and faces Bria looking her over from head to toe repeatedly. Bria could tell, hell anyone with eyes could see, Mark was in a desperate struggle with himself to not allow the lust to penetrate his entire face. He was fighting his best to hide his heart because he knew he wanted her more than just her more than her thorough bred body and cinnamon brown skin. He genuinely felt her Spirit. Ever since Reevah, Mark promise himself to do better. He asked the Universe for not just any woman or another pretty face. He wanted the whole package. To his curiosity he wondered if Bria just might be the answer his prayers finally met.

"Check it out Bria. You got my number just call me when you have some time." Bria rushed over closer to Mark hugging him with tears beginning to swell in her eyes. Mark did his best to hide the emotion and his voice almost cracked from the pressure: "Take care and just text me to let me know at least you made it home safe." "I will. Peace" said Bria as Mark turned and headed out the door leaving her to pay for her books. "Peace Bria." Mark said gesturing with his index and middle finger closed together on his right hand before stepping out into the storefront light and into the darkness of the parking lot. Deuces.

The lateness of the hour brought a nippiness to the air. "Man, I had to get out of there!" Mark said to himself while unlocking the door to his truck. Standing there for a second to gather his cool and enjoy the night he turns to his right to look back at Bria wrapping up her purchase. She so short she has to stand on her tippy toes to reach the raised counter. "Man! That girl is fine!" Mark exclaims shaking his head with a smile. Bria turns spotting him and beams her golden smile and heads out the door. "I thought you left me." She asked innocently. "Nah, I had to get one more look at that apple of yours." Mark is beginning to give in to his true feelings. Bria giggles, "Ah see, you're gonna get me in trouble." "Nah, I just thought I'd wait to make sure you got to your car alright." Mark returns with a wink. "Yeah okay. Thank you Mark." Bria says kindly. "I'll text you when I get in, I promise." She says. "Okay, be safe." Mark replies and they both hop into their vehicles pulling off, red lights go this way red lights go that way.

## Chapter Nine: Signs Before A Fall

After a good meal and a movie, not to mention plenty of cognac, Mark calls it a night. He decides to lay it down. But on his way to the bedroom he checks his phone for messages finding none. His fingers press the side of his iPhone locking the screen. He thinks for a moment, "Bria is full of shit. It must be a good thing or a sign from The Creator she hasn't texted." This way at least, he can say he avoided the temptation of another beautiful sister who couldn't wait to drop more baggage and drama on him. "Shew! Man cool." He lays the phone down on a table.

The beige walls in Mark's hallway leading to his room were golden with a standing lamp attentively at the back corner of the way to the left of the entrance leading inside his bedroom. The hardwood floor squeaked a little but it was clean and comfortable. Mark's rugged copper toned bare feet stepped across it firmly. He paused to look over the paint job he'd finished a few days ago and shook his head approvingly up and down. His dark brown eyes roll over the trim of the four doorways leading to a dead end of the hall where his sister's titanium lamp stood highlighting an original dark olive complected Moorish "Emir" painting. The Emir, dressed in pristine white linen complete with matching turban with golden silken fabric wrapped over leading to a sash. The Emir's style is immaculate down to soft cloth crimson with gold designed flats on his feet. "Man I did pretty good." Mark says after saluting the painting then yawning as he enters his room of amethyst decor. Actual stones seem to float in mid-air by the walls where they sit atop small cherry oak wall mounting shelves. Amethyst to his right twinkles in the dimly lit room; a lavender chalcedony sphere rests across the room to his left. The air of Frankincense spreads throughout.

Mark glances at the wall to the right of his chalcedony at the picture of his family affectionately before plopping down on his king size Tempurpedic. It doesn't take too long before the last whiff of Frankincense swirls above him gently closing his eyes. The meditation cd he put in over an hour ago plays just loud enough for him to hear it clearly. "Ala la wa Ayah wa pa Ayah…Awam Ayah… Aummmm" the man and woman chant uniformly. "Aummmm" the room and smoke from the incense dissipate. "Awam Ayah" Mark smiles like he's in a whole other realm. "Ala la wa Ayah wa pa Ayah" Mark sees a blue six pointed star, then a red one! Then an…Ancient Phoenician *Alif*… Mark's face makes a curious expression. He can't figure out what he's seeing or where he is. Now, suddenly, all he hears is the peaceful voice of a woman but he can't see her. He knows he's moving closer to her but he can't see a thing—it's too dark. Like indigo. Mark can sense the woman is very close to him but her voice is the same tone just a bit more audible. He turns comfortably on his left side and his body language tells him he's in deep sleep. Delta; The woman's voice says:
"Long, long ago when sunbeams struck the North Gate enhancing the solid gold construction…The salt in the

mist had become familiar during the unusually long voyage. During the battle everyone on board suffered minor to serious injuries. Thank God they made it out alive with no real damage done to the ship. Fortunately, the Kaliph was wise and sent extra food and supplies in his graciousness. There's no need for the map now. Everyone onboard knows exactly where they are and the sight of beautiful white flowers grow clearer and larger with each rise of the tide. The ship sails ahead on the crystal blue waters. A hint of orange offsets the air, the crew abounds with smiles and gestures of relief. The Emissary picks up a well known song filling the spaces between the rising and falling of the ship and the waves. The mockingbird perches on a blossoming branch excitedly from the land of flowers. It's as if the small black eyes recognizes this particular ship as it reaches port. Leather burgundy Moroccan styled shoes grace the pier three steps before a quick shadow is cast on the wood by the approach of a bright white pillar of light as the Emissary prostrates. The navy blue tassel of his red tarboosh flitters in the gentle breeze just when he rises and heads towards the Mufti and thoroughbred stallion awaiting him. "Salaam akhi." The Mufti salutes. "Yahshalawam akh. Ma shalawam ka?" The Emissary responds. "I'm well. I see you've taken fire, is the empire in jeopardy?" The Mufti inquires of the concerned look from the Emissary. The Emissary doesn't reply but mounts his horse and they make haste on their journey to the capital city.

The green hills and mounds of earthen works are blurred as the two travel with furry. The inhabitants of the land intuit the desperation behind this sight speaking through the tailwinds of the Emissary and Mufti's speed. The stallions grunt and blow steam out their nostrils at their top pace, stretching their powerful legs, covering miles at a time. Through a wavy haze the center fountain of the city comes into view. There are multitudes of turbans, tarbooshes, and feathered headdresses complementing three-fourths of cloth of all hues going about their business.

A guard spots the blur from the tower as it transforms into the plain view of the Emissary's red and Mufti's black tarboosh. The guard signals the other officers and the two official's horses slow to a slight trot, then walk. They dismount and are formally escorted to an area closely resembling Hala Sultan Tekke. The Emissary and The Mufti salute the Emperor bringing their right hands over their hearts as they enter: "Salaam Shahanshah." They greet the Emperor in unison. "Salaam akhayim. What news from my cousin?" The Emperor asks candidly. "Shahanshah, I'm afraid the invaders from the Cold Mountains have spread. They have breached the iron walls to civilization. He would ask for reinforcements but the infidels now know our trade routes as well as the way to your majesty's dominions here in the North Gate. He fears the days of your dominions filled with peace and prosperity shall be brought to an end through bloodshed and war. There are traitors who have aided them in reaching your borders and now have settled on your majesty's mainlands."

"I see." Said the Emperor contemplating his Emissary's message. The smoke from frankincense burning permeates the sunlit room. "So is this the trouble which delayed your return as well as injured your arm?" He asks the Emissary. "Kahn Shahanshah, indeed." A mockingbird lands on the window sill facing the direction of the Emperor and sings a little. Everyone's attention is turned towards the small black and white bird--only for a moment. The Emperor smiles appreciatively then turns to his Emissary, the Mufti, and the rest of his men...thunder suddenly booms in the distance! "So...it is war then." The Emperor commands solemnly.

## Chapter Ten: Intrigue & Carelessness

Now you see what I'm saying about demons? I mean Mark still didn't know what was going on with that silly assed chick but his Spirit knew something wasn't right. That's what the war was all about in his dream. I've heard him call them Jinn from time to time. Demons, Jinn, or whatever you want to call them were right there sharing the same house and bed with me!

This leads me back to the point of meeting my half brother for the first time and trying to develop a relationship. Unfortunately, our mothers didn't get a long. A lot of family secrets were revealed as he began to come to all of my basketball and football games at PHS. Around this same time I started to get an understanding as to why he hardly returned our father's calls. My biological father seemed to always call me when it came time to cut his grass or do some other kind of labor around his house. Whenever I visited him I noticed some of his family as well as his wife's relatives didn't really like me too much. I didn't feel comfortable. In retrospect, what I found crazy was that my pops told me that he should've married *my* mother. What's even crazier is that my brother is still upset with our pops for not leaving us anything after he passed. He felt that because he tried to stop by and keep up or checked on him that he should've been thought of in a higher light and left some kind of inheritance. However, my father decided to leave everything he owned to his wife. I didn't trip. I had never asked him for anything before and he really hadn't offered me anything either. Whenever I did get to visit him I called prior to just showing up. His wife always seemed mean to me. She tended to grieve or raise hell whenever I asked my father if it was okay for me to stop by. She was evil. She hardly spoke to me whenever I did stop by, never offered me food, and my brother had to even bring her rude behavior to her attention during one visit. See, Terry wasn't her child either but he was around my father and his wife more than I had been.

Yeah, so after lil bruh told me about his dream I was kind of stuck between intrigue and carelessness. I did my best telling it back to y'all. Not that I thought he was tripping but I was just happy to be away from that crazy lying ass bitch. Although the complete road to my recovery was long ahead, I began to feel the warmth of the security in finding myself and remembering my purpose again. Slowly but surely, my thoughts shifted into to the past. I recalled how Mom, Gabby, and I had moved from Lincoln Courts in Over-The-Rhine to Winton Terrace.

The lights were off. From what I remembered I was about six years old. This is around the time I started to play organized football. I didn't really like it that much but BB, Lisa, and Gabby pretty much pushed me into playing. They and the rest of the basketball coaches and parents and guys from the neighborhood who played at Paddock Hills kept telling me I wasn't tall enough for Basketball. I didn't care what they said though. I kept playing both. All I wanted to do is go to either the NBA or NFL and take care of Moms and my family. Moms would always say, "It's all in the Lord's hands baby. Either way, you're the best!" I'd smile and hug her because she was happy. I loved seeing her happy. She had that same smile on her face at church too. It just so happened that during one service I glanced across a couple of pews and up into the choir stand and saw one of the cutest smiles I had laid my eyes on beaming at me. I turned to the right then left before I realized the gorgeous brown skin girl with black hair in the same style MC Lyte had in her video Paper Thin, wearing a red blouse and black skirt with a booty out to here was batting her almond shaped eyes right at me!

I saw her a few times at Saturday School. For those who don't know Saturday School was what our church called Sunday School but because the church membership had begun outgrowing the building space we had our Bible lessons on Saturday mornings instead. On the following Sundays our church had two regular services one was the Early Morning Service that started around 8am which most of the youth and young adults loved because it went faster and the other was the 11am Service which usually could last past 2pm. Both services were packed and we often had visiting churches come with services that began around 4pm not to mention First Sundays when we'd have communion. Some Sundays we'd literally be in church all day and into the night! It wasn't uncommon for Mark to be at both the early morning and 11am services plus any afternoon services at our church or visit those churches ours fellowshipped with. I'm so grateful my Moms didn't make me go through all that. I don't know how Mark did it! But anyway, back to babygirl.

From nowhere Karina started sending me notes during Saturday School class. Like I said earlier, I used to notice her looking at me during services and wondered why. I tried to ignore her but as stupid as it sounds, I don't know why because she was fine. We're talking good, gracious, and mercy fine! Dewayne, Mark, and I were all in the same class with her too. Mama Kendra was our teacher so we had to be on our best behavior and slick. She didn't play. If she caught us passing notes in her class, not only would she have verbally called us out on the spot but she also would have also made sure my Moms and Karina's parents knew every single detail! The whole run down plus, she would've taken the note and read it out loud for everyone in class. Finally, to top that off, she would somehow incorporate Bible verses to substantiate our wrong doing and need for repentance! I thank the Higher Power tremendously that Mama Kendra didn't catch Karina and I.

Her note read, "Hi Freddy. I know we're supposed to be listening to Sister Kendra but I just wanted to know if you have a girlfriend?" I quickly slid the note in my Bible and looked up as Mama Kendra's voice inflected. She had turned and faced the class having wrote a scripture on the board. "Does anyone have any questions?" She asked while she gave the class a polite look over. "I do!" Dewayne grabbed everyone's attention. "Go head

Dewayne." Mama Kendra stood nobly and held her hands in front of her. She was tall, fairly slender, and always dressed to a capital T. A highly intelligent, beautiful and spiritual woman. A real one. I'm glad she and my mother were very good friends. For real like sisters. "Sister Kendra. So when God calls us it's a sin if we don't listen. Right?" Dewayne's chair squeaked as he adjusted and kind of wiggled himself to its edge. "Mmmhmm." Mama Kendra kindly responded. Dewayne wiped the building sweat on his forehead with a yellow Los Angeles Lakers rag that matched his Lakers sweat suite. Man he loved the Lakers. That's another story. Let me stay on point...

"Well God's calling me now Sister Kendra. Can I go to the bathroom please?" Mama Kendra and the entire class roared with laughter. I breathed a sigh of relief as Dewayne walked out and the class began to settle back down. I glanced over to Karina who seemed to have expected me to. The dimples in her round cheeks made her look just like a babydoll. I shook my head from side to side. Her eyes lit up with disbelief. Her notebook pounded to the hardwood floor. "Okay class. Let's get back to our lesson." Mama Kendra gave Stacey a stack of handouts we passed around the room. Karina and I never broke our stares at one another while we received and passed the papers to those on each side of us.

## Chapter Eleven: Karina Maxey?

Maybe that next Sunday or so Karina's father Rev. Maxey invited me to dinner. I was scared of her father. He was stout or maybe to be more accurate, a bit plump with "Chinese" eyes and had a solid gold front tooth. At first glance he'd put you in the mind of the chubby Buddha. Mr. Maxey looked like he kicked a whole lot of ass in his day and still wasn't ready to hang it up! Most of the time he didn't smile. When Karina introduced me to him and her mother Mrs. Maxey, she and her mother walked off leaving me and Mr. Maxey alone. "You alright son?" Mr. Maxey inquired. He spoke so fast sometimes it was hard to understand him. "Huh? Uh, yessir!" I replied. "Oh okay just checking. You seem nervous." I felt like Mr. Maxey cornered me. So never being one to back down to anyone I told him straight up. "You look like you done knocked a few brothas out and don't mind doing it again Rev. Maxey. I gotta be careful with you." I offered with a smile. Mr. Maxey's big belly jiggled. His rowdy laughter carried on like your loud uncle does when your auntie clowns your other uncle for getting in trouble when they were little and ended up getting a whooping when all he asked for was the hot sauce. Mr. Maxey's laughter caused the remaining church members who congregated inside the sanctuary after the 11am Service that Sunday to turn in our direction. "Don't be scared of me unless you're doing something wrong. Are you doing something wrong?" Rev. Maxey's gold tooth sparkled with a keen smile but I knew he was serious. "No sir. I don't want Nooooo trouble. Not at all!" I replied with a straight face which caused Mr. Maxey to laugh even harder.

Around this time Karina had made her way back over to us and wrapped her arm around her father's. Rev. Maxey looked over to her and they both smiled like twins. "Daddy, I want him to be my boyfriend." Jokingly, Mr. Maxey head snapped back and Karina made a play sad face then the two of them giggled. Shit. I was casing the sanctuary for the nearest exit. Karina had caught me completely off guard with that one. I couldn't tell if Rev. Maxey was okay with Karina being that serious about a boy plus standing there right in front of the altar? Rev. Maxey kissed his daughter on the cheek and offered me his hand. "Nice to meet ya brother." He said with his belly still jiggling with laughter as he walked away.

After I got to know him we laughed and smiled a lot. Whenever I went over their house for a visit Mrs. Maxey always gave me food. Always. We would finish dinner or a snack and she'd say "Would you like some cake?" Mrs. Maxey was for sure trying to put some meat on my bones! "Sure. I'd like some. Thank you." I'd reply respectfully. While she walked into the kitchen I heard Mrs. Maxey tease Karina, "Guurrrl he's a keeper!"

The Maxey's were good people. Sometimes they even picked me up and brought me back home from their house whenever I didn't have a ride or change for the Metro. Karina and I dated from the seventh grade until the end of my freshmen year at PHS. Everything was good until I made a pop up visit to Roger Bacon High School to watch a basketball game.

## Chapter Twelve: Fool Me Once

Gabby always loved being different. Hell, we both do. So when it came time for us to move from Winton Terrace to Sharonville, she decided she wanted to go to Roger Bacon. Moms asked if I was interested in going too but I wasn't. I was cool on Catholic school and having to wear the same thing everyday. I was good knowing I was going to PHS and being able to completely be myself.

From time to time Moms and I visited Gabby at Bacon for games and different events she participated in after school. We were at the Roger Bacon versus Purcell Marian's basketball game. Gabby and I sat in the bleachers fairly close to the court watching while I teased her throughout the game as she jumped around and yelled "Gooo Spartans!" She sounded all proper when she did it, cheesing like a Subway commercial. In the middle of the two of us laughing, I looked across the gym and noticed a lot of heat coming from off a face that a few weeks prior sat outside my mother's house with his cousin trying to get at Gabby that one way.

First off, please don't forget. Karina and I were on very good terms. She didn't give me any reason to suspect she wasn't happy with me or our relationship. Her parents and little sister Vet loved me. We spoke pretty much everyday and saw each other just about every weekend including after church on Sundays. As a matter of fact, she and I had hooked up earlier that same day before I got home before I ended up bumping into this dude.

As I walked down the sidewalk leading to Moms' apartment two dudes jumped out from behind the evergreen bushes on either side of the front door. "Yeah that's dat nigga!" One of them said. "What up bruh? Y'all sure y'all at the right house?" I asked scoping both of their body languages. The one who spoke was about the same height as me with a box top hairstyle and brown skinned. He looked like a pretty boy for real. A sucker. The other dude was dark skinned and stocky. He looked like he could get down. "Man you need to leave my girl alone." Dude with the box said. The other guy started approaching me slowly. "Yo girl? Nigga *I don't know you.*" I returned firmly. "A yo Dash!" I casually called up to my sister BB and her husband's open room window. Before we all knew it Dash's 6 foot 5 and 300 pound frame stood at the front door. The two dudes looked Dash up and down then back over at me. "Now, what you say your name was again bruh?" I asked the dude with the box top politely. "Sean." He said. "And you? Ain't you trynna to holler at my sister nigga?" My attentions switched to the other guy. "Yeah. I'm Gill, Sean's cousin." "Okay. Well check this out y'all… I don't know you or your girl but I'll tell you this…" And before I could finish my sentence Dash rumbled, "Look, Sean, Gill or whatever the fuck y'all names is, one of y'all can scrap with Fred straight up but ain't gonna be no jumping!" Dash had that look in his eyes. He was so big he could've snapped a grown man's neck without much effort. He was agile, smart, and fearless. A sucker's worst nightmare! "Aw man, we was just saying leave ole' girl alone that's all." Sean commented. "Man let's be out." Gill motioned with his hand and head as he approached his gray Volkswagen Rabbit.

Dash had begun walking away from the open door as I stood watching the car's passenger side window roll down then the car slowly back out. Suddenly, I thought "who the fuck is this dude girl?" Gabby didn't even go to PHS and I know Gill didn't either. "Hey man whose yo girl?" I took a quick step from the front entrance and yelled. "You know who she is! Just remember what I told you!" Sean screamed out the window just loud enough to overcome Gill shifting gears.

Later that night Gabby told me that Gill actually went to Woodward. That information made things more confusing and after a long day of classes and practice I didn't have the energy to sort it all through so I ate dinner and went to sleep.

Now Gabby and I were having a great time clowning at the game. Our mutual friend Carlos walked over to where we sat. Carlos and I got cool having bumped into him at several Roger Bacon events. "Oh!" The crowd yelled as one of Purcell's players went up for a dunk and missed. "He almost had dat shit didn't he?" I said. "Sho' did!" Carlos returned with a smile. "Yeah man dude used to tear us up. Dunking all over us every year. He's only a junior too. Been on varsity since he was a freshmen." Carlos explained. "Oh yeah? What's his name?" I asked curiously. "Sean LeDane or…something like that. I

KNOW his first name's Sean though." Carlos shook his head up and down convincingly. "That right?" I kept my eyes on Sean as he received admirable pats and daps from his teammates and coaches while he made his way to sit down on the bench. He took a water bottle from one of the trainers and grabbed a towel and wiped the sweat from his slightly round light brown face then wrapped it around his neck. He looked up and across the gym. "Fred check it out!" Carlos elbowed me in the arm. Roger Bacon's best three-point shooter was open and with ball. He launched a beautiful shot. Swish! All net. The gym went crazy. People from Bacon all stood up in front of us shouting and cheering. So did Gabby. I didn't forget Sean's face though.

I didn't think anything about asking Karina about Sean because I didn't consider him a threat. On top of that, I was used to dudes hating on me on GP. I didn't give him too much credibility or energy. Some dudes, hell people period, can be so insecure. I was known and presently known for being friendly so in my mind dude could've been talking about any random girl he may have seen me simply say hi too.

A few weeks later I went to Paddock Hills to play basketball with some old homies from around the way. The next I know we were balling hard and I got pushed from the back. "I told you to leave my girl alone. She's with me!" Call me stupid, slow, or naive but that's when I put two and two together. Sean went to Purcell just like Karina! She had never told me about dude or let me know

70

she had started kicking it with him or anyone else. In that moment where I gathered myself after he pushed me, I quickly turned around and both the Wildboys and Renegades surrounded us. I squared him up. No questions. "What you gon do b—!" WHOP! WHOP! I immediately bombed on him. No more talking. I landed a couple more shots to his bloody face after he hit the deck. He tried to make it to one knee but my uppercut was just kind of too fast and too much for him to take. He dropped flat and was done. As soon as I got home I called Karina. "Yeah your muthafuckin' boyfriend just came at me again and for *the last time*." She was completely caught off guard. "Wha? Why are you talking to me like this?" She sounded so confused and innocent. She had never heard me talk like that before. "I (pause) said (pause) yo muthafuckin' **-boy- friend-** Sean LeDane who YOU been kickin' it with…I beat his punk ass and you and me done. That's it!" And I hung up the phone. End of story.

## Chapter Thirteen: Kung Pao Chicken

What's funny is Karina's whole family made attempts
to get me to get back with her after she played me.
Seemed like before and after any service, choir rehearsal,
or program one of them was in my face having small talk
which usually ended with them saying how much they
loved me and how sorry Karina was for what happened.
"That's okay and I appreciate you apologizing to me but
nah I'm good." I always said. They slowed way down after
Mrs. Maxey wanted to set up a meeting with her, Rev.
Maxey, Karina, Moms, and me. Mrs. Maxey thought we
all needed to sit down and talk everything out and
hopefully Karina and I could reconcile. Mrs. Maxey
approached Moms and was like, "Sister Rose I'm so sorry
for what happened between Karina and Freddy. Me and
brother Maxey really like him. He's a good son. Brother
Maxey and I want to sit down with you and the two of
them so we can work this out. Praise God." Moms smiled.
She turned to me and asked, "Do you want to meet with
them baby?" Although I liked the Maxeys too, with a
straight face I flatly told Moms "Nope." Moms kind of
chuckled in her usual way when something tickled her
with the truth. She responded to Mrs. Maxey "Freddy
doesn't want to so we won't be meeting. Praise God."
Then she and I walked on about our business. Yep. That
was my Moms. She had the sweetest way of being so
serious. She knew how to have fun but she wasn't
absolutely nobody to play with. Feel me?

After things went the way they did with Karina, I wasn't really into actually trying to be steady with any one girl. Karina got over on me so good I became extra cautious. I was still friendly. I mean, I smiled and had conversations but my eyes, ears, and head were all open and paying close attention. I wasn't going to miss shit again! Then along came Naomi. Damn. Here we go…

It was the middle of my freshmen year. One day I was in a more playful mood than usual when I seen her rocking one of her famous old lady sweaters and flower dresses. We always said hi to each other before Math class started but that day I thought I'd cut up just a little bit. As I walked down the aisle to my seat Naomi looked up from her book. "Will you by my tutor?" I asked. "Your tutor? Freddy please, you don't need my help." Naomi smiled brightly. That was probably the first time I had noticed how pretty she was. I mean we were like 14 or 15 but the way she dressed at that time, wore her hair, and carried herself everybody thought she was much, much older. Honestly, she really did look like an old lady. Miss plain Jane with trifocals. But the next thing I knew we were spending time studying after school, talking on the phone, and hanging out on the weekend whenever I wasn't working.

I had a job at the Wok. My buddy Alex referred me. He wanted to quit so he introduced me to the boss, Mr. Yi, in order for me to take his place. I was paid under the table because I didn't have a worker's permit. Once I learned the ropes, it was on! I learned how to cook everything. Everything including my favorite, Kung Pao chicken. Before long I was opening and closing the store by myself. I was bringing home around three to four hundred dollars every week. That was a nice piece of change for a teenager back then. Mr. Yi was so cool. He always told me, "Freddy. Cook as much as you want. Take home." Shit he didn't have to tell me twice! I used to come home with the jumbo bag full of food. Everybody at the house ate good! Everybody claims I can't cook though. Shit I like it. Strange thing is now after reflecting on being poisoned with Mercury I started forgetting how to cook. Makes me wonder how long I had been poisoned. Had to be very slow and over a longer period of time than I first thought.

With me and Gabby making our own money and kicking in on the bills at Moms house, she hit us both with a blessing not many teenagers, poor or rich, ever get. I came in from work and saw a set of keys on the kitchen table. I sat the warm bag of Wok food down eyeing the two keys that looked similar to the ones I had for our apartment. I shrugged it off and started taking boxes out the bag looking for the fresh and hot Kung Pao chicken with vegetable fried rice. "Hey babe!" Moms greeted me with a smile. I snagged a couple fingers full of chicken in my mouth just before I turned and gave her a big squeeze hug and kiss on the cheek. "Hey baby! You look so good Mama! Love ya girl!" I teased. "Boy you so silly." Moms said as she took a quick sniff and peek inside the bag. "Mmm-hmm. That sure smells good. You know they've invented forks Freddy." She joked. "Did you see your new keys?" Moms asked as she pulled out a box of rice, adjusted her robe and took a seat at the table. "Yes ma'am I did. I figured you might've had the locks changed but I was like nah, I used the ones I got to open the door. Ha!" I basically swallowed more chicken and rice. "You think? No boy, those keys are for you and Gabby's place. I got y'all your own apartment. Time for you to learn more about how to take care of yourself. Y'all doing so good but the best way for you to learn is to do it yourself." Moms was so cool, calm and collected with the way she said it that I just was like, "Well hey! Thanks baby. Love you Mama."

## Chapter Fourteen: Truth Above Everything

It seemed like no sooner than Gabby and I got our new apartment that she started talking to Mello and I first began seeing shadows around people. But we'll get more into that later. For real, we had a new level of freedom where I was began to realize invited a whole lot of potential problems and definite temptations.

One of the first temptations I overcame was after I got home from basketball practice one night. Smooth was chilling in the living room. This dude was literally like silk. Tall skinny and never raised his voice or lost his cool — for real. Seriously, he's one of the few people I've ever known that always kept his calm. Never let people see him sweat and was funny as hell! Shit Smooth was a baller and was good at baseball too. He and Mark were in the same grade and rapped together in a group sometimes too.

Smooth used to stop by from time to time especially when he started hollering at Kim. I slapped him dap and walked up the stairs with my bag in hand, opened my door and closed it. I was ready to relax. My mind was on nothing else but sleep. But this time when I looked up after turning on the light there was Leah butt naked on my bed! Lea was a senior. She was beautiful like candy, tall, and had the body of a thoroughbred. Natural hair and no makeup. Man! She had to realize the utter shock and disbelief on my face as she rolled onto her back and spread her long caramel and hairless legs wide open and called me toward her slowly with her index finger. I was

frozen! I couldn't believe my eyes. I knew she liked me
before popping up in my bed. She used to flirt with me
but she went with my little homie Lenz. Lenz was my
brother's good homie too. I couldn't and wouldn't cross
him that way. He and I always got along and I had love
for him and his parents. Most importantly, real homies
don't violate each other like that. "Girl, you're crazy!" I
told her and slid out the room. Smooth had dosed off to
sleep when I smashed down on the chair across from the
couch where he was. "Man why you ain't tell me Leah was
up in my room bruh?" Smooth yawned and made a
strange face. "Say what now?" He didn't know. "Man did
you know Leah was upstairs in my room-on-my-bed-butt-
naked?" Smooth suddenly grappled the air in front of him
like he was falling in mid air from a skyscraper. He
brought himself to a stand. He was completely awake
now. "Say what?! Leah upstairs naked bruh? Aw wow."
Smooth was so damn cool. Usually, you could barely hear
him when he spoke. But after hearing that news he raised
his octaves a hundred notches! "Man Lenz gonna trip. He
in love with that chick man." I said sadly. "You gonna
tell'em Freddy? Man that's gonna be ugly but he needs to
know who he been dealing with bruh." Smooth was right.
The next day in school while standing in Time Square
with some of the homies I saw Lenz and Leah approach. I
already knew what he wanted. Mark gave me dap and
walked away with Holly just when they were a few steps
away.

It was obvious Lenz was upset. I don't remember if

Smooth mentioned anything or not. I really don't think he did. Knowing Leah she may have painted a picture or Kim may have said something because she came out the kitchen after hearing me and Smooth when I told him. Who knows?

Old girl really didn't seem that bothered at all. Maybe I was trippin' but she honestly didn't seem to care that they were approaching me. I can only guess that she may have thought that I wouldn't tell Lenz the truth in front of her. But after Lenz said "What's good Big Freddy?" I already had my mind made up that I was going to let him know the deal. "Hey, everythang good Lenz. What's up with you mane?" Now usually, I'd be smiling wide and bright but I didn't think with the bomb I was about to drop on my homie called for me to do such so I kept a calm look and waited for what I knew was next. "Hey bruh I'm not trying to put you on front street but you always tell me the truth so I gotta know for myself, was Leah in your bed Freddy?" Leah smacked her lips then rolled her eyes. Lenz was so humble and cool. An all around good dude. I hated him being in that position but without hesitation or second thought I looked him straight in the eyes and told him, "Yeah man. She was. She was there before I got home and when I turned on the lights in my room there she was butt naked. I told her she was crazy and went back downstairs." Leah exhaled like she was frustrated and started to walk away. It looked like her whole face morphed or changed colors like she was a whole other type of being. But not human. Lenz hung his head for a split second before he walked her down and basically cussed her all the way out. Later, maybe a week or so had passed, and Lenz stopped by my house and thanked me for being real with him. He wasn't mad at me at all. Even after he asked me if I had hit and I told him the truth that I didn't. To my amazement he felt like I should have on the fact it would have proved how much of a true hoe and disloyal she actually was. "Nah bruh. Real ones don't get down like that mane. Plus, I don't want it if it's that easy. Shit, if she'd do you like that she wouldn't hesitate to do it to me eventually. Feel me?" Lenz and I slapped dap and went to shoot hoop with Smooth and some of the other homies.

When we got done balling I started putting my sweats back on over my shorts. I leaned against the fence cage that surrounded the court. It was getting darker and the court lights were on. We only had a few minutes before the boys came through shining their flashlights from their patrol cars telling us to go home or get taken to jail. While I slid on my pants, a cold breeze blew by a few feet away from me from nowhere. A few leaves were swirling nearby but I don't know where they came from. There were no trees near the court or the recreation center. At least not close enough for their leaves to get over the fences. They would have had at least the length of a football field to travel. But their they were swirling. Everybody had already started walking into the darkness towards their bikes and cars which were in between the light posts along the sidewalk heading out of the basketball court gates. "C'mon man!" One of the homies called out. I thought I was the only one left in the court but when I finally got my sweats on and picked up the rest of my stuff, I looked up and saw this funny looking white dude. That's the best way I can explain him. He had what I think was a black trench coat on with what looked like some J's. Brand new Jordan 1's. I'll never forget that. He was standing in the middle of the court with his back towards me but I know my J's! He had the first ones. Suddenly, the leaves fell flat to the ground. Dude started rocking back and forth and front to back. Like he was at a prayer wall or something. "What is you on, dude?" I thought to myself. I thought he was a geeker. A fiend you know? So I shook it off, took my Gatorade out my bag and took a swig. "Whatever." I said and was almost through the gate when I heard…"Hmmmm Oh, hmmm." I turned around and there was like a dark pillar or cylinder where the dude was before I walked away. Maybe that was where the humming came from? Shit, I don't know. But I was tripping because dude wasn't there! I leaned forward and…nothing. I mean I couldn't even see the red of his shoes. I don't know. I turned to walk away and got in the car. I looked back at the court and dude was standing there with his back still turned towards me. Like he reappeared or….shit I don't know. That shit was crazy. "Man, that's some weird shit. Fuck is in this Gatorade? Mark would love this shit." Skkkrrr. I got the hell on.

I loved messing with Tales about Tierra. He was infatuated with her. I used to hang with Tierra, Veronica,

Wanda, Mona, and Belinda. They were some of the finest girls in school. So I said fuck it. One night after I dropped Mark off at home I turned the corner and stopped over Tales and Loopy's. Seemed like it was darker than usual that night. I mean it was about three in the morning and I sort of giggled to myself as I started down the street towards their house. I could see Mama Kendra's light come on from the back of the house. I knew Lil Bruh was in for it! At that point, he didn't care about getting beat with whatever Mama Kendra had nearby or slapped repeatedly in the face. I felt sad about it at the same time too. He wasn't perfect by no means but Mama Kendra never cut him any slack.

But anyway, as I cruised down the street, I suddenly noticed two small sets of orange like flames ignite over by a dimly lit driveway car port. I was a little tired and my vision became a little blurry as I tried to make out figures. It wasn't a big deal for people to sit out under their carports or the front porches or backyard decks and have a smoke while talking or listening to the radio. That's how it was in Woodlawn and the Zone. But I couldn't see anything. No arms, legs, nor heads. I was tripping! In the daytime I never hardly paid any attention to that particular house besides the fact that the grass seemed to always need to be cut and during winters no one seemed to shovel out the driveway. "What the fuck?" I said to myself as the orange light rushed up to the sidewalk and revealed some weird, dirty looking nigga I'd seen around the city before. His whole vibe was off. Standing there staggering with a half full bottle of Old English in one hand and a blunt that reeked of some other shit I couldn't make out but it was so potent the scent came through the moonroof of my car!

We made eye contact for a brief second. Just as the headlights of my car illuminated his thin but solid reserved frame. He seemed like he had just vomited or was on the verge. Just as the lights could completely shine on him, he and the orange flame were gone! I grabbed the rearview mirror. Both sets of the small orange lights were gone and the house was pitch black. "Say what? I know I'm sleepy now." I said to myself as I made it to the corner of Tale's street and pulled up to his house. Just the thought of telling him I had spoken to Tiera earlier that day was enough for me to completely drown out what had just happened from my mind. He was so into trying to fuck her that he couldn't think or talk straight. Nobody could barely understand that fool when he talked anyway plus, I knew that nigga would not have believed me if I told him. He would've said I was drunk or had smoked too much weed myself. I hadn't done either that night at all.

When I got over Tale's house they were doing the usual. On the phone and playing Playstation. It was some little random hoochie over on the couch staring blankly at the changing colors on the television. She was cute but said nothing when I spoke, "Hey how you doing?" She gave me a plastic smile just before she popped the green bubble gum she chewed. "Dummy can't you speak?" Loopy barked at her. "Boy shut up! I don't know that nigga." She said. "Don't pay her no mind Freddy. She stupid." Loopy said with a chuckle. "Fuck you! I ain't stupid!" She screamed. With the phone stuck between the side of his face and his shoulder Tales laughter sounded like a burlap bag full of sharp rocks. From upstairs Miss Irene yelled, "Hey y'all need to cut that noise out! It's 3 o'clock in the morning!" She was right. They were always so disrespectful to their mother and her husband. I didn't want the chick. I laughed at her. She looked like her self esteem was so low that everybody who lived on Loopy's street or was cool with him had got with her. She was one of the first of many crew pieces those dudes kept around. In other words, she shared herself with everybody we were cool with or knew. Community property man. Sad.

## Chapter Fifteen: Me vs Everybody

So I said fuck it man. I'm tired of people asking me questions but not accepting my answers. I had had enough of the bullshit. It was what it was with Leah. It was like some of those niggas over in the Zone had a issue with me just because they had problems with their girls giving me more respect than them. Talk about real live demons. I don't know what came over ol' girl but she wasn't the first or the last I'd see morph like that. Shit, Karina didn't even look the same after what she and her dude pulled. I was really feeling her too. Man all this makes me think about a dream I had not too long after that twilight zone episode with Leah.

It was on the weekend. A Saturday night after one of our hoop games. I came back home and pushed play on my boombox. That thing was extra cool! Better and bigger than the one LL Cool J had on his album cover. It was all black and around four feet long and just about two feet high! The speakers could slide apart on both sides of the adjustable EQ dials and it even had an extra two notches for Super Bass! Man that thing was tight! Moms even got Mark one too. Anyway, I pressed play on the cassette player. I don't remember where I got this mix-tape from but it had the long version to the Art of Noise's song, "Moments In Love." As soon as I heard the beat I pressed rewind and it stopped at the beginning of the song. Oh yeah, my boombox could do that too. As the

percussion started to fade in I slid down on my bed
stomach first and stretched my arms underneath and
between the coolness of both my pillows and sheets. That's
one of my favorite feelings when the pillow is cold along
with the part of the sheets just under it. Snap! The sound
of the song's finger snaps took me out smoothly. Then the
next thing I saw was a stone doorway. It had to be mid
afternoon judging by the way the sunlight highlighted the
massive stones making up the room on a certain angle that
allowed a shadow to be casted just under the doorway
entrance. I stepped slowly through the corridor where
torches rested on their posts alternating on my right then
left every three or four feet. They must have been there
for after sunset because there would have been a fair
amount of light without them for that time of day. I didn't
know where I was but it was like I felt like I actually did. I
was calm and collected. Curious but not stressing the fact
that I was in a whole other time and place. After several
minutes of walking straight ahead I came to a wall with
golden holes that looked like a wine rack for a lack of
better description. The small spaces were filled with
scrolls. As I got closer to examine what were at least fifty
separate scrolls there was a soft tone which resembled
microphone feedback. The strange thing was the tone was
not annoying or disturbing. It was almost as if it was
beaconing me to turn towards my right and continue
down another corridor. From there it was like as soon as I
decided in my mind to go down the corridor, a jaguar
suddenly appeared on a raised platform a few feet to my

left. I stopped dead in my tracks! It purred. I mean it was chillin' with one paw resting over the platform's edge. It yawned and moved its head around a little, and then let it to rest on top of its other paw. Yet, it never lost eye contact with me. WOOOONG...WOOOONG...I faced the direction it seemed where the tone was coming from and cautiously took a step. The jaguar yawned again apparently saying to me, "Fool, I ain't tripping on you. I'm good." So to be sure I made a few quick steps on my tippy toes like Moms was looking for me and headed past the jaguar further ahead.

There were torches on both sides of this corridor and a darkness that seemed miles ahead. I thought to myself how is that possible? I'm inside. How big is this place? I kept going forward as more and more torches continued lighting the path near me but the darkness was still ahead. So far ahead. In an instant it I was passing by gold and silver relics I've never seen before not even in History class. They were all spotless like they had been cleaned and polished very recently. There were more golden holes but on both sides of the corridor this time. However, instead of them being full of scrolls some were empty. A gust of wind and the flames of the torches dipped black and then bright again. WOOOONG…WOOOONG… instead of the tone feeling like it was coming from the direction in front of me now it seemed I was completely surrounded by it. I turned behind me and the darkness struck me straight in the face! The torches to my sides were still lit and shining. I slowly turned back towards the corridor in the direction I was going and the torches were all still going strong. "I know I've been walking for a minute but it's still so far to go to get to whatever's passed that darkness ahead. Am I still inside? Where am I?" I just kept repeating that as the tone now felt like it wanted me to. Each time it sounded I felt a warmth in the middle of my chest. After continuing on for what seemed like miles the tone started to make sense. Like it was talking like a person. Strange right? It was like inside my mind and had a voice like a woman or something. I don't know who the woman was but that's what it kind of sounded like. And then it stopped! I was in complete darkness. While I was walking it was like it would take ages to reach it and the corridor was lit up until that point. "What the fuck? How'd did I…." I was turning around and must have looked like a real fool. Like a guinea pig in a cage way too small. I mean, I couldn't see shit. WOOOONG! I snapped my head in the tone's direction. This time there was no voice. I started to feel sweat trickling down my

face but I wasn't hot. There was a dripping. DRIP…
DRIP…DRIP but I couldn't tell where it came from. It
was pitch black. I called out "What's up? Somebody
here?!" DRIP…DRIP…DRIP…and it went on and on.
WOOOONG! I snapped my head around and wiped my
forehead. I leaned forward as best I could squinting my
eyes trying to make what these little pinkish or red dots
where in the distance in front of me. Then out of the blue I
started smelling liquor. I know I kept turning around
because it was so dark. I wondered if the dripping was
liquor because it just made no sense to me where the smell
was coming from. The dots were moving now…like a
strobe light and then pulsating from position to position.
From what I remembered they were on the walls of the
corridor one second then the next in mid air in the middle
of the corridor and then it was like they were bouncing
from side to side wall to wall. I managed to put together
that the smell got stronger the closer the dots came to
wherever it was I was, you know? DRIP…DRIP…
PLOP! The moisture smacked me in the face. I felt
around on the ground but it was dry! "What fuck is going
on?" I said. Next thing I knew the two pinkish reddish
dots were blood red eyeballs glaring at me right in the
face.

"Whoa!" My cover flew in the air high enough to hit the ceiling fan. "Moments in love…" I quickly sat up and took a deep breath. The EQ lights on my boombox calmed me back down. I rubbed the back of my neck as my eyes scanned around familiar settings. "Boy that shit was crazy." I laid back down on my back and slowly closed my eyes after counting the fan's spins. Before I got too comfortable I hopped back up and cracked my window to let the cool night air circulate. Before I could stretch back out too perfectly, a cat hissed just below my window followed by a ruffling of the evergreen bush where it must have taken shelter. "Yeah.. we knowzz wer' e at now." I exploded up to my window. "Freddy! Stop making all that damn noise! I gotta get up and go to school tomorrow! I got a test!" Gabby yelled. "Shut up girl!" I returned with a my head on a swivel not letting my eyes off a thing out my window. No one was there. The cat trotted in the parking lot towards a light post and under a parked car in the lot near the sidewalk. A sudden gust of wind and the light from the light post went dark for a couple seconds and right back on to shine brightly. It didn't go back out. I could see Springfield Pike from there and I know it was too late at night for anyone to be walking on that street. There are no sidewalks on that section of the road on either side of the street until you get to Walgreens on the corner. It's enough light to make out someone walking or a dog or cat strolling along. "What the f...?" I noticed something kind of from float over the pavement. I guess it was walking but it didn't have legs! I mean it didn't have a body either. It seemed to be in the form or shape of a human being but it was a dark shadow. I know that for a fact. There were enough street lights on Springfield Pike to make out whether a car, person, or animal was on it! This thing passed directly under a few of them but no one was there!

"Man this is too much for one night." I took out the mixtape and put in LL Cool J... "I feel good...ahh wooo about Kanday!" Then I was out.

Having seniors come over to see me while I was in junior high at Crest Hills, I wasn't new to fame or popularity. I mean girls and dudes. Dudes mostly wanted to fight and tried to jump me back then but when I transferred to PHS that changed. I mean it took awhile. The ladies liked me which made a lot of dudes mad from the Heights. The Smashers originally wanted to jump me and beat me up bad until my cousins DJ and T-Smoke got involved. Some of the Smashers thought I was trying to talk and take away their girlfriends. It was silly really. Plus, the ones who actually confronted me didn't know I had blood relatives from Lincoln Heights. See in those days if you weren't from Lincoln Heights and or didn't have family actually living there or from there and you tried to come to the neighborhood or mess with anyone from there, you would get your ass beat. Point blank. I loved Lincoln Heights. My mother used to bring me out there when I was too small to remember. We had uncles and cousins all through there but unfortunately, some of the Smashers who had a problem with me didn't do their research to find that fact out until DJ and T-Smoke paid them a visit and broke down our family history. Fortunately, that worked but some of the more ignorant ones still had a problem with me because of their own personal insecurities about their girls. That, of course, was not my problem. After my cousins and I cleared up my family ties, and I explained that I didn't want their girls, some of those dudes still had problems with me. I couldn't figure out why. I remember coming down the hall in school one day and they gathered around me and Reese and G40 looked out for me. "Do y'all even know why y'all trying to jump Freddy?" Reese said. E-Dollarz yelled, "It don't matter!" G40 replied, "Y'all niggas dumb. Leave that man alone. He plays football so he's all good." I was glad Reese and G40 said something. It helped a lot. I had grown sick of trying to take the high road. I was ready to use the martial arts training on each one of them that day.

My first day of football practice at PHS I was excited

and had looked forward to being on the team. Unfortunately, some of my new teammates didn't think I was good enough to be there. Dudes said things like, "Man he came all the way over here from Woodward for what?" G40 even told me directly, "You gotta prove yourself here man. So far it's looking like you ain't got that shit." So I said, "Okay." I started running through everybody even him and he was an All-State linebacker. I told myself, "You got to assert yourself and let these niggas know! Turn that shit on!"

Everyday in practice I felt threatened like I had to not only prove myself but also protect myself. I was taking shots from some teammates who were members of The Smashers who tried to test me. "I'ma get you." E-Dollarz told me one day before practice then lo and behold, he blindsided me after coach blew the whistle and I blacked out. That was the first time I ever had my bell rung like that. I got him back though. It was on an option play. The quarterback had the ball and I led the way to the cornerback. E-Dollarz came up too early and he didn't realize it before it was too late. I smacked him head on and plowed right over him! "Ooooooooh!" Everybody said. Coach Fox our Defensive Coordinator cursed him out. "How the fuck y'all let him come up in here and do you like that?!" I laughed and smiled so hard on the inside. Coach Fox was not to be played with. Looking back on my running style now several years later, that day probably is what changed my mentality. Prior to coming to PHS and running the ball, I used to stop and start, putting moves on guys instead of just running through people. That season I realized and embraced the fact that it was all about power and running through muthafuckas. I mean my running power and toughness became my talking. I wasn't a shit talker or a kiss ass like Pete Miller. He was the other competition I had in the backfield. Besides politics, Pete used to kiss the coaches asses. I wasn't from none of the neighborhoods that made up the PCS District so I had to work extra hard to standout amongst my peers. Pete was from one of the neighborhoods but I don't remember which one. He knew everyone and everyone knew him. He was good too so I couldn't understand why he felt like he needed to kiss the coaches ass for playing time. Maybe he felt like I was too much competition. However, I was not nor ever will kiss anyone's ass for no reason. A lot of the time I felt like because I didn't kiss ass I was being ignored and overlooked so I decided to concentrate on beating out everyone I could with my talent and let that talk for me. It finally started to work after I ran over and through our starting defense on many occasions in practice. Through it all I still didn't feel completely accepted though. I mean we're talking about being a part of a team where mostly all the brothers on the team were literally related and or had known each other since birth plus were from the same neighborhood. And, as far as our white teammates were concerned, they had grown up with them or had known and played with them since sixth grade or junior high. Especially if the brothers were from Lincoln Heights. It was a lot to adjust to but things started to come around.

## Chapter Sixteen: Up From A Coma

Like I said before a lot of the brothers from Lincoln Heights didn't accept me. That all changed when I started playing hoop though. I came from a hoop school and played with some of Woodward's legends like Chip Jones, Orlando Williams, and DJ Boston. My luck started to change with the homies after I hit the winning shot against one of our rivals Hamilton High at the buzzer. I caught the inbounds pass and came up the court. We were down by a basket and the clock was ticking down. I pulled up quickly at half court and took the shot... Swish. The crowd went wild! All my teammates ran up on me giving me high fives and dap. After that game on the weekends and during the Spring and Summers I started to get invited to play down at Lincoln Heights Elementary School's gym by my homie Stacks. We called him Stacks because he stayed with a pocket full of money. Feel me?

It was funny going down to the gym with Stacks. Everyone else from The Zone didn't know I could ball so Stacks always picked me to be on his team. During those games I played so well that Stacks and I usually won most of them so the homies started wanting me on their teams and after we finished playing they started opening up and talking to me. They wanted to be cool. "So did Woodward have bitches?" Was a regular "ice breaker" with some of the homies from The Zone that I started to get to know. I mean that's just how some of them talked. It tripped me out because just a few seconds ago while we were hooping they were fouling me so hard and actually shoving and pushing me into the concrete and stage walls of the gym. It was crazy because it wasn't until I was in the tenth grade that all the homies at PHS started being cool with me.

With those new friendships also came more interested girls. First there was Trina Gavin. Trina was thick boy! She had hazel eyes and was like a homie for real. We used to watch sports and hang out over each other's houses. She loved to watch me play ball and actually kept up with my stats! Up until then I hadn't met a girl like that. But Trina had game. She was messing with some dude that went to Withrow and didn't know I had people there. They told me one day that they saw her and dude together. If I remember right, she might have even went to their school to visit him and they recognized her. I had to let her go. I wasn't about to be nobody's fool. I won't lie though, breaking up with her hurt a lot. I thought she was my friend for real, you know?

Next there was Falana Huffington. She was tall and red bone. Falana had the body of a grown woman at like 15! She was known for her pretty eyes and very impressive jugs. Man she was fine! I apologize y'all. Lil Bruh tells me all the time I need to stop sounding so vulgar. I don't mean to offend anyone especially the ladies. I'm working on it and I will do better. But Falana and I kicked it around for a little. She lived in the same apartment complex that I did. Falana was cool and everything but she had a dude who she kept claiming she didn't want nothing else to do with but somehow dude always found his way in the picture. I mean he was popping up over her house, calling her while her and I were on the phone, or coming up to the school. I got tired of that shit and had to tell her we couldn't be together. "I don't need that kind of drama." I said. "But I told him that I don't want to be with him. I told him to leave me alone." She said. "Well obviously, your message wasn't clear enough for him. I ain't got time." I replied and we never hooked up again even though she kept trying. I just got tired of her games.

And then there was Anisha Jones. Man that girl was so fine! Just like the song by Mint Condition. But I didn't trust Anisha as far as I could throw a elephant. I got that shit from Lil Bruh. Man she was a cutie pie for real. She dressed so fly and had as many sneakers as any of the homies. I mean she had a pair for each and every outfit she sported. I'm saying every color too! She had all kinds of Guess Jeans, Gennerra, you name it Anisha had it. She was a dope girl. Literally. She had way too much going on for me. I wasn't necessarily tripping on her being in the game, she was doing her best to help her parents pay bills but what I couldn't handle was how many dudes I saw her juggling. I didn't trust it at all. Anisha was one of those chicks who KNEW she looked good and knew how to work it AND she had mouth piece. Man that girl could talk a lion out its mane, mane! She always came over my house unannounced or called me at odd hours just to check on me. Man one time she got butt naked for me because I was sick and offered to give me sexual healing because Marvin Gaye came on the radio! I know some of the homies thought I was so stupid for not getting with her. But hey, I didn't and I think that was another reason why she kept coming on to me stronger and stronger. Anisha didn't care who I was involved with at all. Even when I started to like Naomi my tutor and we decided to become official. Anisha kept flirting and trying to "get a piece of me" as she loved to say.

Now Naomi she was exactly my speed. She was just what I needed and was looking for. She was super smart and kept to herself mostly. I mean she had friends but her and her friends were the easygoing quiet types. They didn't dress provocatively nor did they seek to bring unnecessary attention to themselves. Naomi helped me because my grades were struggling after coming to PHS from Woodward. The curriculum was a lot tougher and it took me a minute to get adjusted. I remember the first time I really looked at her. I mean got a real good view of who she was. Naomi always wore these old lady like dresses with all these flowers and stuff on them and also wore these thick glasses. On the day I finally realized that I liked her more than just a tutor or friend, she had on one of those old lady dresses. Man she looked like a pilgrim or something but she had a bump! "Hey what's that bump back there?" I asked before we took our seats in the library. Naomi looked all around. She was confused and intrigued. "Where? What do you mean?" She replied curiously and all the way naive. "Oh, you gotta butt!" I said with a smile. She blushed. "Oh wow!" Naomi replied bashfully. "Take those glasses off. Let me see you." Naomi looked down slowly and then carefully took off her glasses. "Aww man, you're pretty." I said. And she really was. I don't think nobody really knew how beautiful Naomi was with all those old lady dresses and those glasses she wore. I mean she really was a nerd but super down to earth and sweet. "You think so?" She said. "Yes. Do you wanna go out on a date?" I asked Naomi as we gazed into each other eyes. "A date? People go out on those? I mean, you want to go out on one with me?" She asked. I giggled. "Sure. Let's go out. Wherever you wanna go." I assured her. And just like that we were inseparable. Before I knew it the haters started pouring through the flood gates. I could see them a mile away. They had colors to them. Some had black shadows and dark forms near them whenever they approached us. I don't know where the ability to spot them came from but all I can say is that I can remember seeing them after I blacked out that day in practice. Sometimes they smelled funny too.

Naomi and I were out shopping when a guy came near where we were looking at clothes and he just stood there staring at the both of us. It was weird because he had a blank look on his face. I did my best to ignore him and Naomi seemed to pay him no mind so I kept cool. I bought her some new gear at that store and after we walked away from the register I turned back to see if the dude was still standing there and he was! He had the same blank look on his face only this time it was like a dark spike of light or energy was coming from out the top of his head.

An olive complected hand presses firmly against a clipboard. A golden pen scribbles madly across a sheet of paper. He stands over a food tray. He's of average height with a stern face. His eyes quickly glance over his silver frames then back down to a form. The sounds of paper switches places on the clipboard. The pen pauses and then a click… "Patient 11172; observation day 17 after admission; vitals normal; weight loss extreme not severe; appetite returning; blood test results adequate for release; no fish or heavy starches; still no conclusive determination as to cause of condition; referring to specialist upon release…" click. "Good morning Dr. Arkelian!" A bubbly middle-aged woman with brown eyes and blonde hair wearing teal scrubs enters. Dr. Arkelian faces Maxine RN. "Morning Maxine. We're all good to go here."

Here I am laying here with these folks poking and sticking me. Demanding blood and piss and it's not a damn thing I can do about it. As many times as they've been in and out of here I already know there's nothing they can do. I know they don't know what's going on or what happened. We're both in the same boat. Stumped. "Okey-dokey sir. I'll let him know when he awakes and get him ready for release." Maxine states. "Mhmm, have a good day now Maxine." Dr. Arkelain replies putting his tape recorder in his jacket and heads out the door.

These folks must be about to come in here for another piece of me. It's getting kind of cold. I'm about to ask the nurse for another blanket if the two she gave me don't start warming me up. Let me just…Freddy struggles to move his leg dangling from under the off-white blankets furled all over his hospital bed. He accidentally kicks the tray table while trying to lift his arms to pull the blanket over him. "Oh! You're up? Good morning, Freddy! How are you today?" Maxine inquires warmly. She walks over and carefully places Freddy's leg back onto the bed and tucks the blankets snugly all around him. "I'm gonna lift your arm up just a little here, okay?" Maxine adjusts Freddy's arm so she can finish tucking him back under the covers. "You're really a good nurse. Maxine, you're better than most." I wanted to let her know I appreciated her. She really was the only nurse during the time I even realized I was in the hospital. She actually seemed to care. The others had attitudes or acted like they didn't want to be there. I didn't understand why because based on what most of the ones who came in my room told me, all I did was sleep and try to eat. They'd get upset that they had to help me to the bathroom or change my sheets because I was too weak to get up and walk on my own. Besides that I didn't ask anyone for anything. "Ah, why thank you Freddy! You're a charmer. My good news for you is… guess whose going home today?" Maxine offered with her usual smile. "Whose picking ya up?" She asked. I drew a blank. "Home? Go…I'm going home, today?" I didn't know what was going on. The nurse's words were clear but they could've been in some ancient dialect for all I knew. I think it was the week before that I woke up to some dude in a suit telling me to sign some papers. He said I had been served. I don't remember who told me but I think it was another nurse or someone who worked with the hospital. Whoever that person was read them and explained to me they were divorce papers. They also went on about insurance. Questioning me about how was I going to pay for my stay? "Yeah, you're going home today Freddy. As soon as we can get the paperwork processed you're free to go. Don't you have family coming to get ya'?" Maxine was matter of fact even though she asked a question. "Uhm...yeah. Yeah, I have family." I told her. I wasn't too sure who was going to pick me up because no one besides Regina and the kids knew I was there. If I remember correctly? I think. I believe I told Gabby or one of my older sisters who also lived in Cincinnati. I really don't remember. I promise I wasn't like this before this particular stint in the hospital. Hell, I wasn't like this even leading up to going to the hospital but some things I guess were missing in my timeline now as I look back on it all. But I do specifically remember when the nurse told me that the doctor prescribed for me to see a Specialist and that I was not supposed to eat any fish or heavy starches.

I think Sandy, one of Regina's associates or Marshall, a good friend from college, ended up picking me up and dropping me off. Actually, Marshall picked me up from the hospital and Sandy met us at my place to help me get settled inside. Okay. I apologize. Please forgive me for my memories being so spotty and all over the place. What actually happened was Regina took me to the hospital in the first place. She also came to pick me up when I was discharged. After being discharged Regina took me to what looked like a bungalow camp. I had driven past this area before I got sick. Back and forth to work or handling errands but didn't know anyone who actually lived there. She pulled up and into a parking space that was just ahead of the sidewalk leading to what ended up becoming my place. Marshall, Regina, and my oldest daughter helped me into my wheelchair and into the bungalow. I was too weak to respond or express the confusion that filled me. Regina and I were in a bad place in our relationship but prior to my stay in the hospital, we still lived in our house together. After a week of being in the hospital and being treated the doctors could not figure out what had happened to me. Regina had somehow moved all of my things out of our house, paid for a few months of rent upfront, and moved me into this bungalow.

I wasn't there at that bungalow for more than a week before contacting Gabby. Next, she and Mark came up to take me back to Cincinnati. It was probably a couple weeks after moving back to Cincinnati that I saw the Specialist who told me that I needed to be admitted to the Emergency Room due to the condition of my blood. While in the Emergency Room with the Specialist, I was again admitted into the hospital where after a couple days my older sister Belinda gave me the divorce papers Regina's lawyer had drawn up and sent to her house. She didn't know where I was after I left the bungalow. Eventually, she realized if I was anywhere, Belinda would know.

Laying there in the hospital the second time opening my eyes as Belinda and my niece came through the day softly saying, "Hey Freddy Fred," I began accepting the reality that Regina had all this shit planned out for a good while.

## Chapter Seventeen: My Incredible Moms!

This leads me back to Mark's old situation. He and that chick Bria started talking more often on the phone. He told me he fought hard as he could from falling for her because not only was she younger than he was but also because after the bad luck he's had with women starting from high school then two baby mamas, he just was sick of getting with the wrong women. Somehow, he said, Bria made him feel like she was different from all the rest. Unfortunately, because of his optimistic heart, Mark couldn't see the red warning signs going off all around Bria. She was used to having a lot of male friends and was the type of chick who hung out with other girls who weren't as attractive as she was in order to standout and get mens attentions. She was looking for a come up if you asked me. Bria had a cool job but had dropped out of college claiming she couldn't pay her student loans. If I knew Mark, and I do, he probably was laid back about that and never said anything about it. But Mark never forgets anything! Seriously. That dude was blessed with a memory better than any computer and can give you details on things you and I would never be able to remember even if we got hypnotized! But anyway, Mark and Bria started talking and he really let her inside his heart in a way he hadn't done since we were in high school with his high school sweetheart Holly. I felt so bad for him while he told me the story about how he allowed Bria to move into his renovated house with him. He even went to the apartment she had been sharing with the dude she was living with and packed his brand new truck up with her belongings and moved her in himself. Yeah, bruh fell hard. I don't think they were six months into the relationship before Bria wound up pregnant. I shook my head as he filled me in on what had happened. He seemed so different. More serious than he'd ever been before around me. I mean he was usually a joker and silly when we kicked it. Not that he wasn't still serious but with me he took a little off the edge you know? He let his guards down because we're brothers. The results of him dealing with so many betrayals in his life, coming back from Cali because of what happened to his sister, plus ol' girl, turned him cold. Like he couldn't control it around me anymore.

"Bruh, this bitch had the nerve to tell me she ain't know how her ex got my address! She talkin' bout her mama didn't give it to him and she didn't either. How the fuck do a nigga in the pen get yo address and the dude in maximum security? He ain't have no special privileges. I grew up with his brothers and sister, so we knew each other but I hadn't spoken to any of them in years Bruh! Then all of a sudden she moves in and he sends mail addressed to her to my house? Fuck outta here man." Mark explained. I shook my head and listened. "She gave that shit to that nigga man." I said. "Bruh, I already know. The bitch is a pathological liar. But it's my fault. The same way you get'em, the same way you lose'em." He said. "You're right Bruh." I replied. I couldn't say anything because it was the truth. Mark knew he should've left the chick alone that night at the bookstore. But he was lonely and thought two years of praying for a "wife" were finally being answered. That's when he said it. "Bruh when I first met her at the class she had a blue light around her. Sometimes it flickered silver to black, so I knew she was trying to balance her spiritual life with the physical world." I sat back in my chair and took a pull of my clove cigarette. I closed my eyes as my little brother stared angrily into the distance beyond my patio tree. He was already used to seeing peoples lights and Spirits and stuff. I got the sense that he was more frustrated in himself for being gifted with the ability yet feeling cursed at the same time because it's so hard and rare to find someone, especially a lover, whose the same way or gets it. Mark was ready to give up on life. He used to love making music, film, and being creative but couldn't find financial support for his ideas. He was a beast though. He learned the law and all the ins and outs of the music and film industry. At that time he felt like The Higher Power had forgotten about him because of all the bullshit he went through growing up and in trying to have a real relationship, family, and a career he really enjoyed. He was tired. "Bruh, I was cooking, cleaning the house, maintaining the landscaping, getting her car fixed, and helping our daughters with their school work plus spending time with them. I loved being a family man. Fucked up part about it, the only thing real about it, besides my girls, was me." Mark's words hit home and deep. I opened my eyes and lit another clove. I started thinking about what Regina had done to me. She had planned the entire relationship. I mean it was all planned. A game and I was a mark. Her target as soon as I started to recognize what was going on. As Mark and I sat out on my patio enjoying the breeze, my memories of my junior year in high school came to mind. The mercury poisoning had done such a job on my memory. I was so grateful lil bruh put me on to the natural remedies and supplements. For real a lot of the conversations about his life when we were away helped to spark memories that had faded or I thought I had lost because of the poison.

"Baby, when it seems like life is completely tearing you down and apart. Don't give up! Don't strike out! You get quiet inside yourself, focus that beautiful mind of yours and stand in front of the mirror. Look at yourself. Smile at your self. Use the energy from all you're going through and direct it through your eyes. When you feel it build up to the point you have to let it out…tell yourself YOU will NEVER destroy me! YOU can't beat me! I'm the CHAMPION! I always win! I already won! Now, you repeat it over and over and over and don't lose eye contact with yourself. See, WE are the Eternal Ones. We are NOT these bodies. This 3D veil program was put onto to us and then manipulated by a small few of our relatives. The 3D experience wasn't meant to be the way it is now. Always remember, the difference between being related and being family."

Moms' reply to Mark after he told her about one of his

dreams came to my mind after Belinda and Niecey left.
We were at her house one day and he came over because
he really couldn't talk to Mama Kendra about too much
outside of church and corporate business type stuff. Shit
Mama Kendra would literally smack him or completely go
off on him for anything she may have felt or thought was
out of the boxes she lived by or understood. She wanted
him to be bougie or a preacher so bad but Mark was never
having it. My incredible Moms. She was one of the few
people who accepted and loved him as he was.

I glanced at those divorce papers and had enough
energy to flop them back onto the chair where Belinda
had sat near the bed. "I gotta get up out this bed." I told
myself over and over. But at that point I couldn't.
Whenever I had to use the bathroom or take a shower the
nurses had to bring the pan or pick me up and put me in
the wheel chair. I didn't have enough strength to reach up
and hold myself up with whatever you call that thing that
hangs over the bed in hospitals. It pissed me off each time
they wheeled me inside the bathroom where I sat so low I
couldn't see myself in the mirror. I thought it was fucked
up that the only time I could catch a glimpse of myself was
when the nurses helped me to sit down on the toilet just
enough to catch the hospital gown before exposing my
bare ass. "Freddy it would be much easier with a catheter
sweetheart" One of the nurses brought up.

I wasn't fooling with no catheter. I told them I'll figure
out how to get to the bathroom without sticking that shit
in me! Shit, I told them they could cut a hole in the

wheelchair and put a bucket under that muthafucka for all I cared. Yeah by that time I had enough of being in hospitals.

At that time some hospital rooms still had phones. Mine had been ringing from time to time but I didn't pick it up. I wasn't going to be billed extra on top of what I knew I was going to owe for not only the Specialist but also this second stint in the hospital. The phone rang again. I rolled my eyes over my left side and saw the little red button blinking and thought to myself, "Whoever keeps calling must have really loved whoever was in this room before me." But then I remembered…I wasn't in Fostoria anymore and it might have been Gabby, Mark or some other family in Cincinnati I didn't mind talking to. But then the ringing stopped. It was too late to try to figure out how I would answer. The night stand was too far away from the bed anyway so I hit the button on the remote dangling on my bed and called for the nurse. BEEP.."Nursing Station. Can I help you?" A nurse replied. "Yes, can you have someone move the phone in my room closer to my bed please?" I asked. "Sure. I'll be there shortly," the nurse said. "Thank you," I replied. BEEP. It was like as soon as the beeping went off letting me know the call ended the nurse came in with a smile and easily slid the stand so close to my bed where all I had to do was extend my arm and pick up the handle.

After the nurse left the room and I adjusted the bed so I could sit completely up, I rested my head back on the pillows and thought about my situation. How did this happen? Where did I go wrong? How could I make things right, you know, get myself better? I'm no saint by any means but I knew full well I didn't deserve the position I was in. Or maybe I did? I kept going over and over things in my mind trying to piece together all the times I may have actually seen Regina making my food or drinks without paying attention or just looking past it. Nothing stood out. But when the Specialist told me it takes a long time of ingesting Mercury in small amounts for it to do the damage it did for someone who was in my condition. It made complete sense in words but since I could not pin down one time where I noticed Regina sliding a teaspoon of swimming pool chlorine in any thing. We did eat a lot of fish and seafood though. Mark used to tease me about how much I ate it. "Damn nigga, you might as well get a cot and ask'em if you can live up in Red Lobster." I mean I'd buy it from the grocery store, go fishing and bring a few back and sometimes Regina's people would bring us some whenever they did the same. I remember asking the Specialist, "Dr. Dogon are you sure it's Mercury? I mean, I've heard of iodine poisoning but doesn't Mercury kill fast?" Dr. Dogon stood about 6'5 with a lean figure like Michael Jordan. He was like how some people say "blue black" his skin was so dark. His dark brown eyes had a shine to them like dude in Master Killer The 36 Chambers movie after he finished the Vision Chamber. They were like he could see flesh and blood, auras, and all that shit at the same time. Sharp as a falcon. "That is correct. A large dose of Mercury ingested at once will kill you however, would that not be something that is so obvious to avoid detection? Does it not make more sense from a diabolical standpoint, for a killer to remain undetected while their victim deteriorates slowly over time? A little here in your cereal a little there at dinner, allowing it to appear as a natural degradation." Dr. Dogon explained. "Damn Doc." I returned flatly. "A rather wickedly wise notion, wouldn't you agree?" He said. "So subtle and almost no way to be traced back to themselves. How could you or the police prove it? You said you don't have a swimming pool but you did happen to notice a small container of chlorine one day in your laundry room, wasn't it?" He asked. "Yes I did. I was on the way out with the kids. I think I was taking them to Chuck E. Cheese or something. Walked right by it and didn't really think about it. I came back home later that day but it was gone. It was a long time before I started feeling bad or sick." I told Dr. Dogon. "Meanwhile it was eating you alive from the inside Freddy. Slowly taking over your blood and mental faculties. In this case parts of your memory. I'm sorry." Dr. Dogon finished. The whole time we spoke his face never showed any emotion at all. His eyes did. If that makes sense? Must be a doctor thing. He was a very unique individual that Dr. Dogon. I've never met anyone like him.

## Chapter Eighteen: Snakes vs Serpents

When Freddy first told me what that Specialist said I was mad as hell! He probably already told you I didn't have anything negative to say about his ex when we first met. How could I? I didn't know her at all and it had been more than five years since Freddy and I kicked it or hung out. I was just glad to see him and know he was alright. He was taking a big step getting married and after his mother passed it seemed like all the bullshit he had dealt with after that was over. He was happy and I wanted him to know I supported him. Regina seemed nice. She was definitely one of the finest Fostoria had to offer at the time. As far as I knew bruh was doing great snatching her up. But when he started going into the poisoning and I had to picture how all of it went down I wanted furniture rearranged. Feel me? I called Amir while Freddy sat there breaking it down and when he picked up Freddy's eyes damn near popped out his head once he heard me say, "Yeah man, it's a quick swoop on and off 75. Trees all over. Shit get lost that way all the time." And hung up. "Bruh what the fuck is wrong with you?! Y'all need to cool out. All the way out!" Freddy mustered enough bass in his voice to let me know he wasn't with it. "Man that's fucked up what she did! How you gonna let that bitch ride bruh?! Shit ain't right! Didn't the Specialist say even if you took it to the boys they'd never be able to prove she did the shit? Man you trippin' but cuz it's YOU, we'll hold." I replied but I was still pissed. I hated her from that second on.

Sandy came in. I guess she heard the commotion. The wheelchair squeaked and the wheels thumped against the wall behind Freddy as he did his best calming me back down. "It wasn't easy but I had to learn to let that shit go Mark." He explained. "Man I know I didn't deserve this. The way it went down. But I did things that put me in a situation where she felt she had to retaliate the way she did." He continued. "Like what man? That shit don't make no sense." I returned still annoyed by it all. "Bruh, I stepped out on her. I was messing with other women and it hurt her deeply. To be even more honest...we both were seeing other people at the same time. She did it first but two wrongs don't make it right. Feel me?" Freddy looked over and smiled at Sandy as she sat down on the love seat near his wheelchair. "Yeah ole' girl is foul." Sandy burst into the conversation. "Now c'mon baby. Don't start. Bruh don't get her started." Freddy tried to giggle the shit off and keep us both quiet. "Nah, what's up wit' it San? What happened? What she do?" I asked damn near falling off the couch while I moved up to the very edge of my seat. "I'm just saying, she and I used to be really cool. Good friends or so I thought." Sandy inched over and locked the wheelchair wheel closest to her. "Thanks babe." Freddy said. "You're welcome. I'm tired of hearing it bump against the wall. Now we gotta keep that thing from squeaking. But anyway, Mark that chick is crazy. I mean she was doing the most even before her and Fred got married but we were girls so I didn't say anything until she started doing dumb shit that started effecting the kids." Sandy's tone was extremely serious and straight to the point. She looked me directly in my eyes the whole time she spoke. "I feel you on y'all were cool but how did it get so bad that you're here with my brother?" Freddy busted out laughing. "My bad bruh you know how I am. Shit. I'm sorry Sandy I just say shit. You know?" I leaned back in the couch and took a long swig of my cognac. It might sound strange but I was glad he was smiling again. It had been a long time since I'd heard him laugh that hard. "That's my lil brother boy!" Freddy announced. Sandy just smiled. "It's okay Mark. It's an honest question. We didn't plan this. It just kind of happened after I saw him breaking down and no one up there was trying to help. I mean nobody. People who had been calling themselves his friends, OUR FRIENDS, AND FAMILY! Nobody Mark! Nobody." Sandy emphasized and quickly crossed her arms and legs as her back pressed against her love seat. Turns out she was taking him to rehab when she'd visit Cincinnati and called Freddy pretty much everyday to check on him. While Freddy was in Fostoria, before his first stint in the hospital, she was stopping by Freddy and Regina's house cooking and babysitting the kids. She did the girls' hair. I mean everything. All this was going on while Freddy still was working and taking care of a house where his wife was hardly there. "Damn Sandy. You had to do ALL THAT?! That's crazy." I couldn't hold back. "Bruh what the fuck was wrong with that chick?" Freddy dropped his head as

he shook it side to side. "I told you shit was crazy bruh."
He said. "Sandy was there man. She saw everything going
on and was the only true friend I had. I mean she was a
real friend to us both but I guess things turned sour
between her and Regina because Sandy kept it real and
told her she wasn't right about how she was handling
things and how it was effecting the kids." I sat silently
checking out the scene as the tv served as our
background. "I bet everybody hated on you too huh,
Sandy?" She sipped her wine and smiled. "Yup. But I
didn't care then and I don't care now. Your brother was
and is a good dude. I saw how hard he was working,
trying to take care of all of them and how he was there for
his children. I respected that shit. Hell, quiet as it's kept,
every woman up there knew."

I liked Sandy the more and more she explained what
had happened during the time Freddy and I weren't in
contact. It was easy too. The way she went through every
detail and wasn't afraid of anything no matter how it
might have sounded or how she may have looked to
someone else on the outside. She told the truth and the
whole truth. I began to see clearly that she truly loved my
bro. For real.

## Chapter Nineteen: Everybody's Not Playing

It was the summer after my junior year at PHS. I had my own crib. Things were lovely. A lot more girls were coming for me too. "Hey Freddy! When you gonna let me take you downtown?" Cherry used to say to me and she didn't mean a place. She meant like the song…You feel me? This chick was a senior and I was cool with her dude. Man this girl used to flirt heavy and hard. She popped up over my place and was throwing herself at me but I wouldn't fold. On top of everything I had going on with working, training, and football practice I didn't catch a break from her or other girls that summer. "I just wanted to talk to you. I couldn't really talk to you when I was in school." Cherry told me one day sitting in her car after I got home. I was walking down the sidewalk and she somehow casually pulled in and parked. "Girl what are you doing here?" I said shocked. Cherry got to explaining how she always wanted me but how she couldn't find the right time to do anything without her boyfriend finding out. Cherry was fine okay? But she was crazy as hell and obviously not loyal too! I wanted nothing to do with her.

Coach Manchester kept calling me up to his office to talk and ask my opinions on different underclassmen he was considering moving around and or for starting positions. He also asked me which position I wanted to play. He told me how he thought about moving me permanently to defense as I had played both ways during my freshmen, sophomore, and junior years. "How do ya feel about Defensive End Freddy?" He asked. "I don't have a problem playing anywhere you want me coach but since I've been here and you brought me here to run the ball and that's where I was for most of last season that's where I want to be my last year." I replied. So that's where he put me. "Well, who do you think needs to be at quarterback and the other running back spot in our Offense?" He asked. Immediately I said, "My brother needs to be at running back. Period. Tex A.K.A Showtime can be a quarterback. He can run but he can't throw. We'll have a good scrambling backfield Coach." I said. "We need a passing game.We've always had a passing game." Coach Manchester said. Thing is, he went with Tex as a starter and Lenz was the backup although he was the better passer. Soon after Coach Byrnes, the running backs coach, came into Coach Manchester's office. Coach Manchester told him my suggestion for Mark to run the ball and Coach Byrnes made a strange face. I found out when we reported for camp that strange look on his face was that he and a couple of the other coaches had something against Lil Bruh for some reason. Mark had never disrespected or did anything wrong to any of them. He always minded his business, hustled, and went to class. I remember when I first told about the meeting I had with Coach Manchester. He was hyped! "I'm ready Bruh! I'm ready!" He yelled. Two-a-days started and I told him "You're here now Bruh! Let's get it!" Tex on the other hand, I hand to make sure I broke things down because he was so *Hollywood*. Dude was funny. I pulled him aside one day we hooked up to hoop at Springdale Recreation Center and told him, "Yeah they gonna give you a shot. Try NOT to fuck it up Tex." He was excited but I could tell he was still very nervous.

I played peace keeper during the entire season because of Tex. Most of the homies from Lincoln Heights didn't like him and not many of our white teammates either. He talked too much shit and was selfish. That's why they called him Hollywood. It got so bad that we used to not block at times and let him get rocked by other teams in order to teach him to shut up, be unselfish, and remain humble. One time during halftime of one our games he complained about being sacked and people missing their blocking assignments. I had to let him know. "Everybody's not used to that Hollywood shit dude. You gonna have to tone it down. Start looking out for other people. It's about family out this way Tex. You still new here. All these niggas is literally family or came up from the soils together. You're on the outside." I explained. That was probably the first time it really seemed to have sunken into his big head. We came back out from halftime against Fairfield. It had been pouring raining all night. The offense took the field and gathered in a huddle. Tex said, "Hey guys, I'm sorry for being selfish and acting like a asshole. I just want to win and be the best but I know I can't do that if I don't play like a teammate and give all you guys the same respect I want. I apologize fellas." The guys all slapped him dap and patted him on the helmet. Mark was even good with him after that. I mean he never had a problem with Tex the way Tex thought he did. Tex just didn't understood that Mark always let his actions do the talking and joked around only so much. I mean Lil Bruh always jokes but he never talked shit unless someone else did it first to a point where he shocks you with a hard comeback because he's so laid back most of the time. It throws people off because sometimes he actually means it or actual facts about someone and they can't take it! Tex found this out the hard way after one of our pregame meals. He was at his usual Hollywood Showtime bragging and boasting before the game where he apologized. I forgot what he said that set Lil Bruh off but Mark exploded and almost beat his ass. If I hadn't been there to get between them it would've got really ugly. "Fool you can't see that don't nobody on the team like yo' muthafuckin' ass? I don't like yo' punk ass either! You talk too fuckin' much! And why the fuck you always smiling and showing' yo' teeth off nigga?!" The whole team broke out laughing. He snapped. Man that was a crazy day. I'm glad we won the game though.

So after Tex apologized we held on to beat Fairfield that night and got things rolling all the way up to Moeller week. Honestly, that moment in the huddle began what became the best and last time I had ever felt a part of a real and genuine team. We bonded together on and off the field in a way that later I learned through experience would never happen again. It's hard to explain but I'll try…

❊ ❊ ❊

Sandy, Sandy, my baby Sandy. How do I start? The most loyal woman outside of my mother I've ever met. My true friend, my heart my everything. She was there when I needed her most. When I was literally on my hands and knees fighting for my life. There she was…right there helping and nurturing me like I was a new born baby. I can hear her now, "Hey, you alright? Need anything?" Sandy was concerned about ME. Selfless. She had children of her own but treated me and mine like we were just as special. So delicate yet unyielding in generosity of care, love, and time. Don't get her twisted, she's funny as hell too! She will make you laugh until you piss yourself. I promise! But hey, don't bullshit her or you'll see the fire burn and burn brightly. I have seen her take off on people like hot lightening off a wet cat's ass for trying to play her sideways. Honestly, I really don't know how I would have made it this far without The Higher Power putting her in my life. Sandy, if you're reading this…thank you. I love you.

There I was sitting at the kitchen table stirring up the tea Sandy had brewed for us both. Rays from the Sun poured over the sink between the oak cabinet on each side of the window pane. Sandy had taken her cup upstairs after throwing some lemon and honey in hers. I listened to her soft steps caress each stair as she climbed to the top floor of our townhouse. Then it hit me! I fought it as long as I could trying to block it out my mind, keeping my thoughts preoccupied with healing my body or changing the subject on myself whenever thoughts of Regina and the divorce came up. I had come such a long way. There were so many things I wished I had done differently. There were so many things I wish I would not have said but even more things I wish I had. The idea of another man being around my kids...my DAUGHTERS at that! It's impossible how many times I yelled and cussed myself and the townhouse out. This chick allowing some cornball to be around my kids trying to direct their lives like he has things together but moving in with a woman and her kids. Dumb shit on both sides. On THEIR behalf to be clear. These fools were so bold that she had him come to over our house at the time while I was there and I answered the door! They both really didn't know how close they were to moving on to the next world.

But today's a good day. The tea is just right. The sunrays feel like they're correcting the issues I've been having with my hands and fingers. It's like I can feel the blood circulating even though that's what it's supposed to do. It's different though. There's no difficulty moving them and I don't have to think so hard to move any part of my body as long as I'm in the Sun. Things are still not perfect but I believe in myself. They will be. The plan is to start a little physical therapy and hopefully, get into the pool so I can walk without a cane or wheelchair. Build up the strength in my lower back and legs. Ahhh. This chamomile tea is hitting good today and just what I need to relax and clear my clouded mind. Where's my...oh! There it is! Now, if I can reach my pen...get out the way napkins! Gotcha. How did Moms' say this goes? Oh yeah, got it. Write their full name, the date and time, what I want to happen, and put the paper in a ziplock freezer bag. Remember, be as detailed and specific as possible. I wish I had a piece of hair or an earring or something but hopefully, the words on the paper will do. Freddy glances ahead towards the middle of the table. The bottom corner of a picture peeks out from under a napkin. It's from he and Regina's wedding day. Freddy stands tall with a smile bigger than all outside. All his pearly whites glimmering. He's dressed in a white tuxedo with a royal blue bowtie. Regina holds a bouquet of white and blue flowers next to him. Her face is pleasantly calm. He picks it up quickly and rips it down the middle. Moms' I believe what you told me baby, here we go.

REGINA WINGATE 320 WEST SOUTH STREET, FOSTORIA, OHIO 44830; NOVEMBER 11, 2004: LEAVE ME ALONE. I AM INVISIBLE TO YOUR DARKNESS AND SHADOWS. I RETURN ALL NEGATIVE ENERGIES BACK TO YOU. KARMA COME SWIFTLY. I RELEASE MYSELF FROM ALL SPIRIT TIES CONNECTED TO YOU CREATED THROUGH SEX AND OTHERWISE. I AM FREE FROM THE BONDAGE AND PAIN INCLUDING THE DIVORCE. KEEP MY BABIES SAFE AND PROTECTED THROUGH IT ALL. HEALING IS MINE.

Now just put this in this ziplock bag with her picture and... Zzzzip! Where's my cane? Is it behind the chair? Or wh..."Babe! Where's my cane?" Watch her say it's somewhere in the kitchen. "You don't see it laying over the chair next to you? On the part of the chair you sit on. Lift the tablecloth!" Sandy shouted. Oh there it is. It's getting easier using this thing even though it looks like I had a stroke and the whole right side of my body moves like it's waking up from being paralyzed. Freddy lifts up the cane and stands with a slight slump. He gingerly makes his way over to a beige chest deep freezer aligned with the furthest corner of the kitchen just after the point where the sunlight ends and a slight shadow forms. Freddy lets the cane slide through his hands just enough so he can stick the bottom of the cane into the slot where normally fingers go to lift the top of the freezer open. Whoo! Cold outside but colder in there! Freddy brings the ziplock bag with the paper he wrote on inside it up to his face and says, "I'm done. I'm free. So it is and so it shall be." He takes the bag and puts it as far down into in the deep freezer as he can while keeping his balance at the same time. Freddy simply let's go of the freezer door letting it slam down. BOOP! "Just in time for the New Moon today Moms'. Love you girl! Ha!" Right then the corner of the kitchen where Freddy stood by the freezer began filling with sunlight. For a quick second Freddy was able to stand straight up without his legs wobbling or his knees buckling. He even managed to lift both of his arms above his head and was still able to hold the cane in his right hand. The hum from the freezer got louder like it was transforming into a Lamborghini engine. Freddy holds his stretch and the freezer roared for a good thirty seconds and then just as the healing photons maximized their intent throughout Freddy and the entire kitchen a swoosh of wind blew out and under the nearby outside door! The light in the kitchen returned to normal and Freddy quickly put his cane back down on the floor almost out of breath. He rested his left hand over the top of the freezer door and regained his balance with his right as his cane stabilized. Freddy turned to face the rest of the kitchen behind him. The window was closed. The heater kicked back on just as he realized water from the kitchen sink was running from the faucet.

## Chapter Twenty: One of Nine Gates Opened

As soon as I closed the door to the freezer I felt like I was as taller than Minut Bol with the athleticism of Michael Jordan! It was like Popeye eating his spinach and all the power from it stretched out his arms and legs, making his pipe spin and then he started kicking ass! I smiled like I worked at Burger King and was auditioning for a new commercial. "Babe! Pick up the phone!" Sandy rang out startling me. I was brought back down to normal. I inched over like Yoda in Return of the Jedi to the living room where the cordless rested on the end table. "Got it baby, you can hang up!" I guess the beep when I pushed talk wasn't good enough for Sandy to get off the phone. "Yeah, hello?" I said. "What up bruh?" It was Mark. "Hey, hey! What's up Mark, you good?" I asked. "You over there smiling nigga?!" Mark could tell I was cheesing. We both got a good chuckle out of it. "Nah, you know I'm messing with you bruh. I'm glad you feeling better. Wanted to ask you if you heard anything about ol' girl missing?" He asked. "Missing?" I was curiously thrown off. "Ol' girl, who? What are you talking about bruh?" I honestly was clueless. "OLE GIRL, Bruh. You know we on the phone fool. What's up with who put you in that fucked up spot? That girl!" He was starting to get heated. "Ohhhh you talking Regina bruh? Man, I ain't heard nothing about her being missing. I did hear she started having health problems after her dude got caught and sentenced to 20 years or however long he got.

Fuck 'em." I replied. After saying that Mark laughed the hardest I'd ever heard him laugh. He got so short on breath I thought I was going to have to call 911 and send the ambulance. Then I thought for a quick second and put two and two together. "Hell nah bruh! Fuck you talking 'bout missing? What did you do? I don't want nothing to do with it!" I went off. Mark laughed on and then came back with, "Man you so crazy. I'ma holla at you later. Gotta dip bruh. Love you man." Then CLICK. "If you like to make a call, please hang up and try again." This nigga. I said to myself after hearing the operator recording. I rustled over to the couch and carefully plopped down to let go one of the deepest sighs someone could imagine as the thoughts of what my little brother might have done.

It felt like hours past as I sat there. The television was on but my thoughts had completely drowned it out. My body was relaxed and I can only guess that I had dosed off to a great sleep. After a couple yawns I began to catch whiffs of liquor in the air. I was set to start physical rehab in a couple of days so I couldn't drink. I didn't have the taste for it right then anyway but for the life of me I couldn't find where the smell was coming from. Sandy had taken a fast from her wine during the time I was recuperating. She didn't want anything to distract me from feeling like we were both working to get control over any vices or things that could slow down the positive gains my health was starting to take again. With that being said, there was no alcohol in the house. Nothing. No beer, no wine, no Hennessy, coolers, nothing! But that smell was strong and unfiltered. I sprung up as quickly as I could from the couch and trekked the entire ground floor of our place sniffing like a bloodhound. I checked the pots and pans on the drying rack. I checked the cabinets I could reach without losing my balance or falling flat on my face. I checked the bathroom because we had company a few days before. I checked behind the plants in the living room; behind the television; behind the couch and the back corner where the bookshelf meets the closed end of the patio door.

From there I made my way upstairs. I couldn't take it anymore. I checked all around my office and the upstairs bathroom. Finally, I headed towards the master bedroom where Sandy met me at the doorway. "What are you looking for?" She asked with a smirk and a 'if you ain't found it by now, you ain't gonna find it' look on her face. "You don't smell that liquor?" I returned perplexed. "Liquor? Uh…no." Sandy's eyes circled around the doorpost before she took a few steps back into the bedroom with her head on a swivel. I got my Scooby-Doo on all over the bedroom and closets before I ended up in the bathroom. Let me tell you I sniffed shoes, clothes, and everything in the dresser drawers. Inside the bathroom I looked under the sink and behind the toilet. I was slick with my cane, sliding the shower curtain to one side before I just said, "Fuck it." I grabbed a wash rag and lathered it up with Zest and cleaned my nostrils out. Don't ask. The idea just came to me. And it worked.

❊ ❊ ❊

"Der dat hoe go right der' Ibby!" Sama points with his index finger coupled by an increasingly wicked expanding grin. "M-hmm." Ib replies just as the crash of a glass bottle smashes into the sidewalk where they hover. It shatters leaving just enough of the REDRUM label in tact. North Main Street is doing it's usual business and traffic flows accordingly. Just another regular day in Fostoria. A caramel complected woman of average height and sultry build leaves out of the Kroger facing West High Street pushing a shopping cart full of grocery bags out the into the parking lot. She's a head turner for sure. A few steps and she pauses for a pickup truck with an elderly couple passes by. The pickup slows to a stop and a short woman with all white hair carefully steps out and heads for the store's entrance. Regina checks both directions and heads down the left side of the parking lot just a close enough distance to the cart drop-off. She brings the cart to a stop again but this time she presses her key fob and the trunk of a late model metallic blue Ford Contour pops up.

POW!!! POW!!! BRRRRRR! POW-POW!!!Smoke spews from out and under a brown unrecognizable... hooptie spreading throughout the opposite side of the parking lot as it pulls in backfiring. This thing's barely hanging on. Rust is accented and highlighted everywhere. Gas and burnt oil fumes wreck havoc on the air. A toddler sitting in a shopping cart waiting for her parents waves his hands in front of her face and rubs her eyes dropping her lollipop with a frown. The hooptie gets lucky and drags into an open space on an aisle over from where Regina's parked. BAM! The passenger side door of the hooptie slams shut and a short pudgy dude with black stringy hair pounces out and up the lot heading for the store. Dude's dirty. His worn boots used to be cool. His trench coat too. They may have been brown in a former life but that life was rough and they are not now! "We damn sho can't use his ride!" Ib's face scrounges up. "Dat's fa damn sho! We uh fa sho get caught up." Sama replies wiping spittle from his mouth.

Regina is about done putting her bags into the trunk. The full shape of her apple bottom gleams into the parking lot aisle behind her as he bends over to make room for the last bags. "C'mon Ib. I'll take him." In the twinkle of an eye a dark form streaks into the back of the man who got out the hooptie. His arms stretch for the sky, his head twitches side to side, and he quickly makes an about face and heads towards Regina.

Country music pours out the window of the pickup truck where the elderly man pulls into a space where he has a clear view of the store's front door. Not too far from the shopping carts aligned on the side of it. He shuts off the engine and drops his hand down patting his knee. He pulls out a checkered handkerchief from the chest pocket of his blue overalls and strongly blows his nose. "God A'mighty. Stinks." He says out loud to himself. "I don't give a gotdaayuum…" the song on the radio recaptures his attention with a whistle but then "Aw dammit! Not now!"

The old man barks while interference takes over the radio. In a rush he spins the dial of his 1987 two toned red and black Chevy Silverado's radio dial. A spark bursts from out the radio slamming the old man's body back against his seat. He violently flicks his hand back and forth to ease the shock and get the feeling back into his fingers. The radio interference stops and goes to a commercial. He reaches for his handkerchief as sweat begins pouring from under his fedora straw hat while taking it off. He wipes his head with a yawn and checks his watch when the truck's interior light flickers. "What the..?" The old man reaches for the light and gets shocked again! This time it's like his hand is glued to the interior light cover. His entire body trembles and shakes. There's a bit of smoke oozing in between his fingers and the palms of his hand. Suddenly, he stops and the light goes back off. His hand flops down to his side and he burps loudly. The truck door opens and he steps out into the parking lot with a slight wobble that smooths out as he walks towards the shopping cart drop-off on the passenger's side of Regina's car.

"Too bad Junior's too little to help me with these damn bags." Regina says finally getting the last grocery bag in the trunk as she carefully eases back up so her head doesn't hit the trunk's edge. "Hey! All dat azz ova der gurl!" Regina slams the trunk with a quick glance towards the voice. The Old Man struts over with a two-step and ends up about three feet away from her. He grabs Regina by the arm before she even realizes what's happening.

"Getcho!" The Old Man covers Regina's mouth with the handkerchief and with both their backs to her car's driver's side windows backs Regina inside. Before The Old Man could twist his arms around to get Regina inside she elbows him in his stomach with all her might. A pair of dirty hands extend out from the passenger's seat and snatches her legs bringing her all the way inside the bouncing car. The Old Man slams the door and yanks the keys out Regina's hands then starts the engine. The blue Contour begins backing out. "Get off me! Let me out! Y'all can have the car! Let me go!" Regina screams at the top of her lungs. She tussles trying to wrestle herself free. "Ohh I like dat mouf. I'ma give ya whatcha need in uh minute baby." The Dirty Dude snickers as Regina struggles on his lap. THUMP...THUMP! His elbows thud against the passenger's door and window as she continues to wrestle him side to side.

## Chapter Twenty-One: Due Diligence

The Sun is setting fast. 22-inch chrome blades twinkle and sparkle as the last few rays of light bounce back and forth against the front driver's side of a dark colored crispy clean SUV. As the lights in the parking lot of the laundry mat just off Perry Street and East High Street glow up to a shine, the limo tint laying on all the windows of the Escalade is impenetrable. A freelance photographer would land a full-time gig at CAR&DRIVER if they showed up and got a shot of the scene. Tires profiled to a perfect 45 degree angle, just enough of a puddle left over from a rain a few days ago. The picture is an otherworldy mystical blend of dusk, street and business lighting in a glorious harmony with the paint job, windows and rims. Clean.

The chrome build of a Desert Eagle .50 rests cooly across the leather center arm rest between the front seats. The charcoal and chrome interior pushes out that new car smell because it is. The LEDs on the display panel and gear shifter highlight with an indigo aura as an OG Kush cloud expands. "You see that fool? That's them right there. They got to her first." Through the front windshield a woman is grabbed and forced inside a blue car. CLICK CLACK. "Yeah, you right homie." Amir says. "It's good you doubled back, feel me?" Amir takes his flag and wipes down a gold matte FN SCAR 15P SMALL SCAR LEGACY. He holds it up in front of him and admires it turning it from side to side. His cutting eyes scan the trigger and shaft ready for his inspector's stamp of approval. He carefully lays it to his side with the business end pointed to the floor up against his seat between the door. "We should see cool with yours and this." Amir leans forward and takes hold of a M&P 2.0 Full Size with a silencer. "Damn...you're FN all the way down ain't you?" Amir glances over towards the driver's seat and with a smirk lets out a flat "Ha." He pushes a button and the magazine releases from out the bottom of the pistol. "The suppressor's a Griffin. This toolie, here's a Smith and Wesson big Mark." Mark taps the screen and the truck's engine roars up. The Escalade softly rolls through the puddle without a splash and heads into the Kroger parking lot at the same time the blue car reaches the lot's exit lane. The rear lights of it glow up and waits for traffic on East Hight Street to clear. "Hey homie, you ain't bring yo suppressor? That eagle gone echo in them woods fa sho'." Amir says facing straight ahead as the glow from the Contour's lights suddenly go dim and it makes a left out the parking lot onto the street. "Why you think they headed out there? Shit. I forgot them wetlands is over that way. Especially if they make that right at North Main Street. That left on East North Main Street; then that next right on Poplar." Mark explains as he whips the SUV out into traffic with his left hand. His right elbow rests just near the Desert Eagle that hasn't moved one inch through or after the turn. "Riiiiight. State Route 18 homie." Amir states as the kush smoke pours out through his nostrils.

"Take dis lef on East Norf." The Dirty Dude points with one hand clutching Regina's unconscious body across her chest with the other. The Contour travels about a block. "Take uh right…right here, right here on Popla." The Dirty Dude emphasizes with his index finger for direction. The Contour turns right on Poplar Street. The Escalade cruises a few car lengths behind and does the same. "Yeah they heading to the wetlands homie." Mark checks traffic in his mirrors and coolly leans back in his seat. Amir passes him a Backwood.

After about ten minutes the two vehicles travel on an open highway and after a few minutes the highway bends then straightens back out. A few feet more there's a country intersection and the cars make a right. The country rode and visibility quickly turns pitch black as a thick patch of forest comes up ahead. Even in daylight sunrays can't push through it. It's night now so only headlights make the tiniest minute dent across the pavement if only for a couple feet ahead at a time. "Pull over there homie. I think I see a break in the woods." Amir points his pistol in a direction on the right just ahead. There does seem to be a small glint of moonlight breaking through some trees. The grass there is lush and it appears to be a break in the road. Maybe a bit of gravel or some kind of paved driveway in the faint light. The Escalade hums a steady tone as it rolls over the grass near pine trees amongst the sound of the 22's braying over smooth rocks mixing the whoo's of owls and crickets chirping handling their business for the night.

"Yuh, yuh. Right der', right der. Mhmm." The Dirty Dude nods his head in the direction of a large break between trees. The Moon ripples near the edge of tall grass and in between patches of Hornwort, Cattail, and Bulrushes. "I gotcha." The Old Man wiggles his nose and promptly reaches over to his door panel and holds down the open window button. The window slowly rolls down a quarter of the way. He faces out the window for a moment. "Yeah yo' ass stank." The draft enters the car just enough for Regina to catch the change bringing a whiff of consciousness back to her. Her head struggles side-to-side, she slightly convulses. She mumbles and her eyes roll uncontrollably in her head for several seconds. The Old Man cuts off the car's headlights and it bumps up and down in rhythm with the moist earth beneath. The seats squeak catching the crickets, night crawlers, and other wetland critters attention for a spell. An owl reopens its sharp eyes and turns its head.

"Less git it gone mane." The Dirty Dude opens the

door. Regina wakes up just enough to realize the car has stopped. She slides to the side as the Dirty Dude brings her up on the side of his hip as his right boot hits the ground. "Get off me!" Regina musters a coherent sentence. "C'mon bitch. You gone give us dat wap." The Dirty Dude squirms with Regina's twists as they grow stronger and more deliberate as she tries to fight free. "Mane we got'er. Heere I cum." The Old Man bolts out his door so fast he rips his back pocket out on the edge of the door panel where it latches and locks on the door panel. "No! Let me go!" Regina manages to get one arm free but not in enough time for The Old man to grab her arm. She gains some footing with a squish. The Old Man and Dirty Dude have one arm each. She wriggles with all her might unfortunately, her movements tightens the grapples of both men. "The Old Man's chin jiggles. He mashes his teeth with a lunatic smile. "Stttrrrip!" Regina's blouse tears exposing one of her breasts to bobble in the night air. "Yea yea she wit it! Get on ova heere." The Dirty Dude goes for Regina's legs bringing her up over his shoulder. She pounds on his back with both hands. The Dirty Dude's back sounds like the baseline to the natural wetland night life symphony. CLICK. Regina faces up. A shiny circle slowly revolves into an even darker space between glints of moonlight. "Shut yo ass up. One mo I'ma smoke you." The Old Man points a .45 caliber handgun in Regina's tear filled face. She instantly realizes the actual depth of her situation. The three of them walk towards a few low hanging Bald Cypress and

Willow trees, however, their squishing feet are muted by all the night life.

A couple frogs near the water line hurry and hop from the moonlight into the water. The frogs near the driveway already cut their ribbits short. The smell of tactical cream tickles the whiskers of a calico cat frozen in mid-stride. It crooks its head a second. The glow from its eyes peeled. It's leaning just below the tip of the top edges of the grass blades. Kneeling on one knee, Amir whispers "A homie, I can't be on this grass too long, feel me? These Ones hit me for a cool stack." Mark grins and points around a tree. The chrome from his pistol is muffled against the darkness of the tree and his all black fits. Slowly, it rests against his leg pointing to the ground. They move.

"Mane you can thro' dat trench on da groun. Lay'er ass on it. Do wut we gotta do den wrap huh ass up init when we thew." The Old Man surveys the ground under one of the trees keeping his gun aimed at Regina. "Gone git down bitch." The Dirty Dude lunges throwing her off his shoulders while flinging his coat off almost in the same motion. "Git down heere." He tells her sitting down. "C'mon. Less git dis ova wit." The Old Man guides Regina's trembling backpedal towards the flat black outreach of the trench coat spread over the ground. "I'm sorry y'all. Whatever I did. I'm sorry. Please don't kill me." She says tears turning into a flood spilling over her cheeks and smacking her folded forearms. "Jess take da rest of dat top off and unbuckle yo pants. We ah do da rest on da groun. Now git down!" The Old Man moves in closer and closer to Regina as she checks behind her for fear of stepping on The Dirty Dude's coat. She sobs as she removes the remainder of her blouse. The Old Man seizes it from her hands and takes an extra long sniff with the barrel of his gun ever ready to blow Regina's head off. He manages one eye closed savoring her scent left in the blouse. The Dirty Dude watches laying on his side on the ground motioning with his fingers for Regina. "C'mon y'all please. Don't do this. I got money. Y'all want some money? I got it. It's all yours. I promise just don't hurt me please. Please don't do this! Don't kill m-" Before she could finish The Dirty Dude leaps up from behind her and grabs her by both arms to a body slam. They both land on the ground, Regina is not on top. "Bitch! We done toll you. Threw playin' wit yo ass. Now you gone take dis D. Both of'em." Regina screams but The Dirty Dude immediately tears off a sleeve from his coat and smashes it into her mouth. Regina tries to get loose rustling back and forth with The Dirty Dude rolling over the coat and parts of the grass simultaneously. The Old Man rushes and makes it over to them both just as Regina tosses and turns The Dirty Dude over on his side. It's too late. The Old Man still has the gun pointed at Regina but this time he presses it into the back of her head sliding down behind her. She's trapped. Abruptly, a few critters crystallize with food in their paws and mouth at the sight of the debauchery. An owl leaps to a soar through a collective of nearby trees before spanning across the widest beam of moonlight in the area.

"Man these fools trippin' hard homie." Amir's gaze is distorted with a twist of his head and scrounged up face. "Those ain't people homie. I don't know. Ol' girl probably down for this bullshit. But all of'em can feel this." Mark cocks his pistol and takes off towards the unnatural and heinous scene through the darkness without a sound. FOO-FOO! Pieces of a tree trunk bust apart and split closest to the heads of the participants on the ground. The panting and groaning pauses. "Wut da fuck?!" The Dirty Dude lifts Regina's hair from off his face to get a better look at the tree's new decor. "Don't worry bout dat mane we still switchin' up. Dis too good." The Old Man manages to speak through the sweat pouring from all over while trying to catch his breath and keeping a rhythm. "A y'all need a break." The Old Man startled slowly turns his head. Amir's pistol meets his eyes. "That's right." Mark stands over the Dirty Dude gun drawn. Both he and Regina rotate their astonishment between the dark flags covering the faces up to the eyes of both Amir and Mark. "Can y'all plea…" Regina mutters through a bloody lip and bruised face. "Shut up!" Mark cuts her off. "Please! They snatched me up and y'all gonna let them keep raping me?! Y'all must've came all the way out here to help. Please!" The Old Man quickly covers her mouth. "Hey look mane we got lute da hit y'all off wit." He glances up and over at Amir and Mark. Amir looks over to Mark and shrugs. "Nah we got bidness with her. She tried to take our people out. We just here to do a job." Mark explains. "Dat right? Shit mane y'all wanna taste mane? Ain't shit.

We uh git on out da way." The Dirty Dude replies through a perverted sincerity. "Say homie it's too much talking. We can full speed ahead on all three and hit the e-way. Let's go." Amir suggests and fires two shots to the back of the head and neck of The Old Man. Regina screams through his trembling hands. "Nah don't cry now! You didn't give a fuck when you did yo dirt." Mark spits through his flag. His eye-brows are bent into a vengeful scowl. "Hey mane dis don't got nuthin' da do wit me! Let me go on and..." On the spur of the moment, the Dirty Dude's blood splats over Regina's face and hair. "Stankin' muthafucka." Mark's pistol smokes. "I'm so sorry! Whatever I did I'm sorry y'all. Please don't kill me. Please don't!" Regina begs and sobs. "If y'all going to kill me please let me put my clothes back on. Don't let me die like this." Regina woefully requests. "A homie, I'ma let you handle this. See you at the ride." Amir states taking a couple steps backwards then disappears into the night. "So will you let me put my clothes on please? I'm saying, I got money in my car. I offered it to them but they didn't want it. I got like 100 stacks. It's my dude's. He moves pills and fin-fin. I was supposed to drop it off to him after I left the store. It's yours if you just let me put my clothes on. Looks like you're going to shoot me anyway so I won't ask for my life." Mark looks over at the position where Amir stood. A shadowy figure can been seen in motion between the trees near the empty space where his truck is parked. Mark motions with the gun towards Regina's clothes. Regina quickly reaches for her pants. "Slow."

Mark says dryly. "Okay, thank you." Regina gently grabs her panties along with her pants that are wrapped around them. "Who are these dudes? Why did they snatch you up?" Mark asks kicking the Dirty Dude's carcass to make sure he's deleted. "I don't know. They ran up on me in the grocery store parking lot. That's all I know." Regina explains. "Don't you know that voodoo shit?" Mark asks as his gun follows Regina's every move. "Voodoo? Why you ask me that?" Regina asks nervously. "Just answer the question." Mark jabs. "Yeah, I do. But actually Santeria. My mother and grandmother taught me and my sisters." Regina responds wiping as much blood as she can from her face with her hands. "Well, maybe these two sick triflin' ass niggas are some type of get back from the Spirit World." Mark returns promptly. "I ain't gonna dump on you. Living is the best punishment. You didn't deserve this at all though. You probably got AIDS or something worse judging by these two filthy muthafuckas." Mark explains motioning with the gun for Regina to stand up. "But my shirt all messed up. Do you have something I can put over me?" Regina asks humbly. "Shit you better get that old dude's shirt from under them overalls. And yeah, yeah. You best believe we taking that money too." Mark says in a harsh and self righteous tone. "No problem. No problem. Thank you." Regina continues as she wrestles the Old Man's shirt from under his apparently evaporating body. "That was deep what you said about the Spirits getting back at me. Maybe there's some truth to it." Regina professes as she covers her chest with her arms before the shirt goes over her head. She begins to slowly step away from the bodies. "Like I said. You didn't deserve this. Nobody does. It's just when somebody calls themself dealing in the Spirit World they have to come all the way correct and know what they're doing. We never know how things will turn out once certain doors get unlocked or what kind of entities can be unleashed." Mark explained. "I feel you on that part." Regina respectfully responds. "Hold up. Where's your bra? Nothing needs to be left that can trace back to you." Mark tells her. "I never wore them." Regina says hanging her head surveying what she can make out of the scene around her. Mark directs her to the space between the trees where Amir disappeared into the night.

As their shoes squish and squash through the tall grass just enough between the sprinkles of moonlight the critters of the night nervously continue back to their occupations although a few cautiously gauge Mark and Regina's movements. As the sloshes of their feet spill more faintly into the harmony of the night, the bodies of The Old Man and The Dirty Dude leak brain matter and other bodily fluids. From his stomach the Old Man's corpse continues deflating by the second. His mouth, frozen opened, begins to emit a dark mist visible only by the hint of moonlight in that particular area of the wetlands. It pours from out his mouth on a curve then builds vertically. The shock in his bodies eyes gape as it all melts down. Another owl lands on a thick leafy branch of a tree just above the Dirty Dude's corpse's fascination with everything over him and studies him from every bit of a ninety-degree angle. The owl scoots to the side with wonderment. The Dirty Dude garbles and coughs. A black gassy cloud takes up into a whirl seemingly in a rush to join up with the dark mist that is now strumming the air into a humanoid like form. The cloud doesn't waste time wreaking through the trees branches past the owl. Two small and red flashes glint left and right almost like probes searching for a focus to a full or sustained glow or complete flash.

"Yeah just let me put the code into the radio so the stash spot will open." Regina pushes a couple buttons on her radio and a THUMP sounds from under the glove compartment. A paper bag falls out exposing a couple stacks with $100.00 bills. "See? The rest is in behind the backseat in the trunk." Regina confirms and hands the bag to Mark. "Bet. This don't change nothing. You better thank your Creator or whoever you pray to that I understand. My sister was raped and murdered. I found her hanging from the ceiling in her garage. I'll say this… from this day forward your temple is corrupted. You and your dude will NEVER prosper. You both have harmed the innocent with that bullshit he serves, the way you have mistreated people, the attitude and lifestyle you have lived off of it. To me, you will forever be damned. In the name of all the upright and righteous ones before us AwamaAyah: AYah Mashallah." Mark affirms as he watches Regina carefully grab a larger bag full of money from the trunk before his gloved hand firmly shuts it. The tears start to dry on Regina's face as Mark's pistol leads them further down the lightless path. A forceful draft blasts against the Escalade as Mark closes the door behind Regina. He steps up and inside and nods. With his flag still covering his face, Amir shifts it in gear and the 22's bling off just a bit from the slice of moonlight still available to their position. The zephyr whooshes past the SUV and up through the spaces between the trees. Four small red circles suspend amid the midst in the air. It scans across as the Escalades headlights and fights it's way through the moonless path and on to the highway.

## Chapter Twenty-Two: Progress Feels Good

The comfort I felt while waking up in my bed hearing Sandy's gentle breathing before I actually opened my eyes the next morning was completely and totally foreign to me. However, at the same time there was a space of familiarity that reminded me of childhood. There was an indigo light surrounding Sandy's head to her shoulder just where the sheets covered the rest of her heavenly frame. I couldn't believe all I had experienced that night. Everything I had seen and heard was far above my understanding but I knew it was real. It was like I could fly and soar witnessing the world only a few can imagine. Although the nights can be cold during Fostoria Spring seasons, in Cincinnati I felt nothing but the breeze being softened by the silver light of the sky. There were no restrictions. I didn't need a cane or wheelchair. I felt stronger than I had in years! I could remember details from my life just as fluently as I had lived through them in real time. As I reflect further, last night was more than a dream because something about the air and the light realigned my skeletal structure as I stretched with an expanse I hadn't since PHS. I woke up with more muscle memory than I had yesterday and that's for sure. Shit it might have just been the mattress! Man, I mean my pillow didn't get hot or anything! It remained cool and it was like my body melted into just the right spot no matter if I moved during my sleep or not. My posture was perfect the entire night and I didn't feel any nudges, elbows, or kicks to my right shin so it's a great chance I didn't snore. That's unusual.

I must have been thinking too hard and woke Sandy. "Morning babe. Hungry? Feel like eggs, turkey sausage, and pancakes?" She yawns to a stretch. "Oh yeah that'll work baby! With your sexy ass! Gimme some sugar girl." I always liked teasing her when she first wakes up. "Okay babe." Sandy says flatly as she ties up her robe and starts out of the bedroom for the stairs. "Check it out baby!" I got up and walked over to the doorpost and started down the stairs. "Oh shit! Good job babe! C'mon keep it up." Sandy smiled brightly and goes on down the last couple steps and out of sight. "Yeah I got this!" I made it down three steps without using the handrail. I reached out with both arms against the walls as support and got down to the kitchen just as Sandy poured out the eggs to a sizzle on the skillet. The phone rang. "Babe can you get that please?" Sandy asked while stirring the pancake batter. "Yeah, I got it baby. Whip that shit baby! Whip it!" I encouraged her making my way over to the phone. Our house phone is white but there was a yellowish glow about it. It sat over on the coffee table just in front of the love seat. I eased my hand gently over the wall and made it without stumbling. I picked it up and studied it for a for a few seconds. "What the...?" I could feel a cozy and easy buzzing vibration while holding the headset. "Uh hello?" I answered. "Hi Daddy! It's Niecey." I stood straight up at once and noticed blue orbs circling my feet. They gradually worked their way up my legs, torso, chest and neck. "Niecey! Hey babygirl! How you doing?" The sizzles heighten and dampen. The smells are growing more intense and the ol' gut is roaring up. "I'm doing good Daddy. I just wanted to tell you how sorry I am for how Mom influenced us to treat you so badly. She was tripping. She told us how she messed her life up by everything she did while y'all were married. She said she knows you're unreachable and she can't muster the courage or energy to even try to call you and apologize. Thank you for doing the best you could to take care of us the best way you knew how through all of it. I love you."

I can't explain the thoughts and feelings that gushed through me hearing the second oldest of my daughters explain how she felt to me. "Aww, you don't have to apologize for your mother baby but I appreciate you telling me how you feel. It wasn't you or your sisters fault. I love you too." I didn't notice Sandy had creeped up behind me and wrapped her arms around me just before any tears could flood my face. "Daddy she's not doing very well these days." I turned my head to return Sandy's smile. "What do you mean babygirl?" Sandy kissed me on the cheek and returned to the kitchen. "Well, her dude got busted and locked up. I think he's about to do like 20 years and she's been going to the hospital a lot. Her weight keeps fluctuating in extremes. Her hair is falling out too." I'd be lying if I said I didn't feel some kind of vindication for hearing what my daughter had to say about her mother but it didn't last very long. There was no reason to bask in her troubles and pain. It wasn't worth it.

Plus, Moms raised me better than that. I didn't need the weight on my soul anymore. My Spirits were being lifted each day Sandy and I were together living our dreams.

Niecey hung up the phone shortly afterwards and Sandy and I enjoyed one of the most delicious breakfasts I've ever had. I had a doctor's appointment about an hour or so later. Sandy and I got ready and I met her in the car. My leg was little tired from all the excitement of the morning so I brought my cane out with me. When I made it to the passenger's side and opened the door a bluejay flew directly over my head and found a spot on the shrubs near the driveway. He looked me dead in the face and chirped. I felt like he said, "What up? Everything's going to be okay, you'll see." I smiled and the bluejay just perched there on the slightly bobbing shrub. The bluejay took a quick look towards the front door, chirped again then flew off. I giggled and sat down in the seat as Sandy came outside and locked up.

I was able to lift my legs above the floor of the door panel and get them inside without help today. I got situated and closed the door just as Sandy made it to the car and opened the driver's side door. "Sorry I took so long babe. A man named Paul Barber called and I took a message. He said he's interested in mentoring you in the Insurance Technologies or something. He said he came across your application and was impressed. I told him we were heading to your doctor's appointment so he asked if you can call him as soon as you get the chance." Sandy takes out a piece of paper with a phone number and hands it over to Freddy. "Paul Barber. Yeah, thanks babe." The car door closes and Sandy turns the key in the ignition. A soft lavender glow emits from her silhouette. I did a double take when I noticed it as she backed out. I looked around as we rolled through the streets. Everything seemed more alive and thriving. The sunlight and colors hit hard and in an entirely new way. So impactful. It felt like everything was in perfect tune with the deepest parts of my soul. I had never felt so much life in being alive than along that ride.

Sandy and I got to the doctor's office that faced Hamilton Avenue before you reached Compton Road if you traveled North. At the time it would've been on the right hand side. We made our way up the covered walkway to the building where there was a handle rail where a cardinal landed a few feet ahead of us. "Aww look babe!" Sandy pointed with admiration. "Yeah I see it. A bluejay was in the shrubs back at the house before you came out. Maybe seeing them means we'll get good news. At least that what Mark would say." I said grinning at the bright red bird. He was brave. He didn't fly away until we completely passed him and opened the building's glass door!

Sandy and I made our way inside and our stroll was rather easy for me. I managed up the slightly curved raising staircase of carpeted stairs without much struggle. The stairs were wide enough for the two of us to walk up comfortably as well as gave me enough space to use my cane. Honestly, I didn't have to apply much pressure when I used it. However, once we made it about a quarter of the way to the top I did feel a bit winded but no weakness in my legs at all. Sandy opened the door and we made our way to my doctor's suite.

When we got into the front area there were so many vine plants hanging over and aligning the front receptionists window I thought we had entered some kind of Zen retreat center. There was Afro Lofi music playing softly seemingly from nowhere because I didn't see any speakers anywhere. On the wall to my right was a large mask with red and yellow fibers. There was also a lot of cowry shells hanging from it. It was different from the one on the opposite wall to my left just above a small wooden table where a small indoor fountain rested. There were purple, blue, yellow, and orange colors pouring out water of the same hues. "This is a cool mask right here, ain't it babe?" I said as I studied its shape and artistry. "It's a healing kanaga from my people." Dr. Dogon explained appearing from literally out of thin air beside Sandy and I. "Oh! We didn't know you were here Doc!" I said with a surprise and smile. "That is understandable and so true. How are you both?" Dr. Dogon asked in his usual emotionless face. "We're good doctor. How are you?" Sandy asked walking over to check out the fountain. "Yes. I am well. This is a healing kanaga my grandfather gave to me and his father gave it to him etc. It's been in my family a long time. The one over on that wall is a dama ceremonial kanaga or, mask as those of the Western world have labelled it, and was worn by my father during the funerary rites of my grandfather." Dr. Dogon placed his right hand over his heart as he finished. We held silence for a moment allowing the fountain to speak. "Please enter." Dr. Dogon opened another door and stood to the side. I thought the door was part of the wall. There was no handle or at least I was too blind to notice one there. The three of us went into what we found to be Dr. Dogon's office or study. There were even more plant vines and kanaga's on the walls nearby and in between several bookshelves. "Please be seated" Dr. Dogon requested as he made his way around a nice sized cherry oak desk. His desk was filled with all types of "thinking" trinkets. That's the best way I can describe them. You know the types of stuff you'd see over people's houses that no one's ever allowed to touch? Yeah, well Doc had a lot of those things on his desk. You already know they were in order and neatly placed. There was a metal looking fidget spinning ball I'd call it. A balance ball table that I heard called a Newton Cradle Stress Reliever, a spinning decision making pen thing, and basically all kinds of cool shit like that. "Ah, Jâm dɛ́rnɛ́-ẁn Heru." Dr. Dogon said as he made his way around the edge of his desk. Once he passed it I happened to notice a nice sized bird perched on a perching staff in the corner. "Please? I didn't understand Doc." I said confused. "I see you've met Heru." Dr. Dogon sat and extended his arm and hand towards the corner where his bird peered closely at me. "This is my friend. He is a Common Kestrel species known as Falco Tinnunculus. In common English he is a Falcon." Dr. Dogon softly clasped his hands over his desk as he sat attentively. I have to admit when he spoke about his falcon Dr. Dogon's usually emotionless face carried a small bit of easement to couple the tone of pleasantness in his voice. "What you didn't understand was that I greeted him and told him to spend his day with peace." Dr.Dogon shared. "Oh okay! I didn't even see him there. I was checking out all the trinkets on your desk." I told him. "Yes." Dr. Dogon stated. There was another pause while I stared at his stoic face. Then Dr. Dogon opened the folder that was under his hands. "Greenbomb...Greenbomb... yes. Brother your last blood work and tests came back good. However, you will have to be consistent with your diet and exercise in order to have a full and sustaining recovery. Now, what does this mean exactly? Yes. I recommend you transition over to an herb and plant base diet including fresh fruits. If you still crave meat which is understandable, please look for free range bison, chicken or turkey. No red meat or pork. Worms or better yet parasites thrive in the bodies and flesh of those animals more malignantly than the aforementioned. However, you have a powerful mind brother Freddy. You can make this transition and train your mind to reject the flesh and blood of animals. Bear in mind your younger days of playing sport. Your physical training has imprinted on your cells and DNA. You can do anything you put your mind to and your body will follow, my brother. Dr. Dogon declared.

"Any questions?" So I asked, "What about fish?" I asked adjusting in my seat. Sandy sucked her teeth. "Although personally, I thoroughly enjoy fish, in your case and situation however, I cannot recommend you partake. You should not put yourself in a situation where you can digest bad fish or seafood. I'm not saying that all fish are bad. What I am saying is if you're not the one who fishes out the fish or seafood yourself, cleans and prepares it, and then cooks it personally, I would refrain because that's the closest way to guarantee it is fresh and has not been tampered with. I'm trying to help you remember that YOU have the power to control what you put in your body and that YOU have a role or part to play in regards to your health. Westerners don't seem to know, believe, or accept this fact until it's entirely too late. Everything is a microwave." Dr. Dogon closed the file and glanced over to Heru. Heru shook his wings a little and resettled himself on his perch. "Okay, Doc. Wow. Okay." Was all I could muster as I processed everything Dr. Dogon told me. I looked over to Sandy who was picking with her fingernails. The sunlight seemed to turn up a notch throughout the bay window behind Dr. Dogon's desk chair. He got up, unlocked it, and then opened it as far as it could go. He turned back around and sat. He folded his hands over the file again and then looked over to Heru and nodded his head. Heru immediately took flight out of the bay window in a single swoop! "However, like Heru, you are free to make your own decisions and not follow my prognosis. Yet remember, if you do not follow what I have recommended you, the results and or side effects are your own responsibility. Meaning, we can only help those who help themselves." Dr. Dogon stood up and rested his right hand over his heart before extending it to me. "Be well and go in peace, my brother." Dr. Dogon said as I shook his hand. As soon as I let go he sat back down and put the file he had read from back in a cabinet near his legs. He brought out another one opened it and took a gold looking pen from this fancy penholder on his desk and quickly started jotting things down.

Sandy and I made it back to the car when I asked her if she would stop by the Kroger that was down the street because I wanted to get a jump on some of those fruits and veggies Doc recommended. I knew this diet transition was going to be very new to me and it probably was going to take some real time for me to get completely adapted to it so I decided to start with this Green Drink Mark told me about when I first told him about the Mercury poisoning. It was like a smoothie and was actually called, GREEN

MACHINE. It was a mix of all kinds of fruits, herbs, and minerals. Shit it was like a meal in and of itself! Plus I also wanted to put some minutes on my phone so I could call Mr. Barber back. I wanted to ride, utilize, and capitalize off of the positive flow that was picking up steam in my life. I had a new lease and promised myself to take advantage of it in real time. No procrastination or waisting anymore energy. "There's a spot right there baby!" I damn near scared Sandy as we pulled into the lot of the grocery store. "I got it. No passenger's seat driving babe." Sandy pulled into a spot near the dead end inside the lot. There was a row of tall bushes and the dumpster close by as well. She didn't even turn the car off before I opened the door then jammed my cane to the asphalt. "Let's get it baby!" I moved like O.J. Simpson in one of those old Hertz commercials except with a cane and I wasn't jumping over nothing. But I did hop an oil slick before I reached the fire lane towards the store's entrance. "Alright now! Don't overdo it babe." Sandy called out as she waited for a Brinks truck to pass and after it started to back in just before we got out the car. I was cheesing like it was my birthday and it was about time to blow out the candles on a cake. The truck passed and Sandy restarted in my direction. She skipped just a little when she looked up at me and returned a smile. "What are you smiling at?" She threw those hazel eyes on me. (There's a lot of people with hazel eyes in this story, right?) "This fine little P.Y.T. playing double-dutch to get over here to me." Thanks. I've always been slick with it. We went inside and headed straight for the phone store at the front of the store right next to the Coins-to-Dollars machine. We went up to the counter and I put another week's worth of minutes on my phone. I thanked the cashier and immediately dialed Mr. Barber's number. He picked up on the third ring. "Freddy! How are you bud? Listen, I'm glad you called so I'm not going to waist any more time. You're a smart guy with a good eye for business. We'd love to have you as one of our mentees. Are you available this Wednesday at 10am to start the program?" I didn't miss a beat. "Absolutely sir, I'll see you 10am on Wednesday. Thank you." Mr. Barber chuckled. "That's great, Freddy. See ya Wednesday."

I hung up the phone and did my best thizz dance. "Boy you're so silly." Sandy chimed. We were out in the store heading for the refrigerator so I could grab the juice. "So you're going to start Wednesday, huh? That's great babe. I'm happy and proud of you." Sandy commented softly while taking my free hand. "Thanks babe. I couldn't have made it this far without The Higher Power, you and Mark. He's the one who turned me on to Doc." Sandy noticed the change in my voice as we finally made it over to refrigerator that was attached to the produce section of the store. "You still haven't heard from him or talked to'em?" Sandy asked while I reached over and grabbed up the 64-ounce bottle. "Nah…we lost contact after he and I talked about when Gabby tried to convince him that I should've went into a nursing home. She got mad at him when he told her that I go natural and see Dr. Dogon and

I should've stayed with her or Belinda. I ended up getting that phone cut off because I missed work while I was in the hospital before moving in with Belinda. Knowing him he's probably West Coasting back in Cali. I hope he's alright." I really did miss Mark. I worried about him. He keeps a lot bottled up and we really didn't get to talk about what happened to Regina. I'm grateful for the good he saw in me and tried to do for me especially after we lost Moms. "I'm sure he's okay babe. You know he's a survivor just like you. Wherever he is, he'll land on his feet. Ain't that what he'd tell you?" Sandy rubbed my back through that smile of hers. By that time we made it to the check out. "That's right baby…he may be outta sight but never out of mind. Forever forward."

www.ingramcontent.com/pod-product-compliance
Lightning Source LLC
Chambersburg PA
CBHW051142020726
47501CB00005B/1628